William Shakespeare's Titus Andronicus: A Retelling in Prose

David Bruce

Published by David Bruce, 2022.

WILLIAM SHAKESPEARE'S TITUS ANDRONICUS: A RETELLING IN PROSE

First edition. July 29, 2022.

Copyright © 2022 David Bruce.

ISBN: 979-8201072094

Written by David Bruce.

Table of Contents

Dedication

My father, Carl Eugene Bruce, died on 24 October 2013. He used to work for Ohio Power, and at one time, his job was to shut off the electricity of people who had not paid their bills. He sometimes would find a home with an impoverished mother and some children. Instead of shutting off their electricity, he would tell the mother that she needed to pay her bill or soon her electricity would be shut off. He would write on a form that no one was home when he stopped by because if no one was home he did not have to shut off their electricity.

The best good deed that anyone ever did for my father occurred after a storm that knocked down many power lines. He and other linemen worked long hours and got wet and cold. Their feet were freezing because water got into their boots and soaked their socks. Fortunately, a kind woman gave my father and the other linemen dry socks to wear.

My mother, Josephine Saturday Bruce, died on 14 June 2003. She used to work at a store that sold clothing. One day, an impoverished mother with a baby clothed in rags walked into the store and started shoplifting in an interesting way: The mother took the rags off her baby and dressed the infant in new clothing. My mother knew that this mother could not afford to buy the clothing, but she helped the mother dress her baby and then she watched as the mother walked out of the store without paying.

***

The doing of good deeds is important. As a free person, you can choose to live your life as a good person or as a bad person. To be a good person, do good deeds. To be a bad person, do bad deeds. If you do good deeds, you will become good. If you do bad deeds, you will become bad. To become the person you want to be, act as if you already are that kind of person. Each of us chooses what kind of person we will become. To become a good person, do the things a good person does. To become a bad person, do the things a bad person does. The opportunity to take action to become the kind of person you want to be is yours.

Human beings have free will. According to the Babylonian Niddah 16b, whenever a baby is to be conceived, the Lailah (angel in charge of contraception) takes the drop of semen that will result in the conception and asks God, "Sovereign of the Universe, what is going to be the fate of this drop? Will it develop into a robust or into a weak person? An intelligent or a stupid person? A wealthy or a poor person?" The Lailah asks all these questions, but it does not ask, "Will it develop into a righteous or a wicked person?" The answer to that question lies in the decisions to be freely made by the human being that is the result of the conception.

A Buddhist monk visiting a class wrote this on the chalkboard: "EVERYONE WANTS TO SAVE THE WORLD, BUT NO ONE WANTS TO HELP MOM DO THE DISHES." The students laughed, but the monk then said, "Statistically, it's highly unlikely that any of you will ever have the opportunity to run into a burning orphanage and rescue an infant. But, in the smallest gesture of kindness — a warm smile, holding the door for the person behind you, shoveling the driveway of the elderly person next door — you have committed an act of immeasurable profundity, because to each of us, our life is our universe."

In her book titled *I Have Chosen to Stay and Fight*, comedian Margaret Cho writes, "I believe that we get complimentary snack-size portions of the afterlife, and we all receive them in a different way." For Ms. Cho, many of her snack-size portions of the afterlife come in hip hop music. Other people get different snack-size portions of the afterlife, and we all must be on the lookout for them when they come our way. And perhaps doing good deeds and experiencing good deeds are snack-size portions of the afterlife.

Educate Yourself
Read Like A Wolf Eats
Be Excellent to Each Other
Books Then, Books Now, Books Forever

***

In this retelling, as in all my retellings, I have tried to make the work of literature accessible to modern readers who may lack some of the knowledge about mythology, religion, and history that the literary work's contemporary audience had.

Do you know a language other than English? If you do, I give you permission to translate this book, copyright your translation, publish or self-publish it, and keep all the royalties for yourself. (Do give me credit, of course, for the original retelling.)

I would like to see my retellings of classic literature used in schools, so I give permission to the country of Finland (and all other countries) to give copies of this book to all students forever. I also give permission to the state of Texas (and all other states) to give copies of this book to all students forever. I also give permission to all teachers to give copies of this book to all students forever.

Teachers need not actually teach my retellings. Teachers are welcome to give students copies of my books as background material. For example, if they are teaching Homer's *Iliad* and *Odyssey*, teachers are welcome to give students copies of my *Virgil's* Aeneid: *A Retelling in Prose* and tell students, "Here's another ancient epic you may want to read in your spare time."

CAST OF CHARACTERS

Male Characters

SATURNINUS, Son to the late Emperor of Rome, and afterwards declared Emperor.

BASSIANUS, Brother to Saturninus, in love with Lavinia.

TITUS ANDRONICUS, a Roman, General against the Goths.

MARCUS ANDRONICUS, Tribune of the People, and brother to Titus.

LUCIUS, QUINTUS, MARTIUS, and MUTIUS, Sons to Titus Andronicus. Lucius is Titus' oldest son.

YOUNG LUCIUS, a Boy, Son to Lucius.

PUBLIUS, Son to Marcus Andronicus.

SEMPRONIUS, CAIUS, and VALENTINE, Kinsmen to Titus.

AEMILIUS, a noble Roman.

ALARBUS, DEMETRIUS, and CHIRON, Sons to Tamora. Alarbus is Tamora's oldest son; he becomes a human sacrifice.

AARON, a Moor, beloved by Tamora. Aaron's skin color is black.

A Captain, Tribune, Messenger, and Clown; Romans.

Goths and Romans.

Female Characters

TAMORA, Queen of the Goths.

LAVINIA, Daughter to Titus Andronicus.

Minor Characters

A Nurse, and a black Child.

Senators, Tribunes, Officers, Soldiers, and Attendants.

SCENE

Rome, and the country near it.

NOTES

ANDRONICI: Plural of ANDRONICUS. It is a family name.

SIRRAH: A term used to address a male who is of lower social status than the speaker.

CHAPTER 1

— 1.1 —

The Roman Emperor had recently died, and his two sons hoped to become the new Emperor. Saturninus based his claim on being the oldest son, while Bassianus based his claim on merit — Bassianus believed that he was more worthy than his older brother to be the new Emperor.

Before the Capitol, Saturninus and his supporters arrived at the same time that Bassianus and his supporters arrived. Both Saturninus and Bassianus wanted to enter the gates and climb up to the Capitol. The gates to the Capitol were located by the Tomb of the Andronici.

Saturninus said, "Noble patricians, supporters of my right to succeed as Emperor, defend the justice of my cause with your weapons, and, countrymen, my loving followers, plead my right to succeed my father as Emperor with your swords. I am my father's first-born son; my father was the most recent to wear the imperial crown of Rome. Therefore, let my father's honors, fame, and glory live on in me by making me Emperor. Do not wrong my seniority and insult me by making my younger brother Emperor."

Bassianus said, "Romans, friends, followers, all of you who support my right to be Emperor, if ever Bassianus, Caesar's son, has been gracious and esteemed in the eyes of royal Rome, then guard this passage to the Capitol and do not allow a dishonorable man to approach the imperial seat. Instead, be dedicated to virtue and to justice, continence and self-control, and nobility. Let desert and worth prevail in a free election, and, Romans, fight for the freedom to make your own choice."

Marcus Andronicus arrived, holding the Emperor's crown. He was in the Capitol, looking down at Saturninus and Bassianus. Marcus was a Tribune and the brother of Titus Andronicus.

Marcus Andronicus said, "You two Princes, who strive by factions and by friends ambitiously for rule and authority, know that the people of Rome, for whom we act as a special party and whose interest we represent as a Tribune, have, by common voice, in election for the Roman Emperor, chosen Titus Andronicus, who has been given the surname Pius — which means pious,

2

patriotic, and dutiful — for the many good and great deeds he has done for Rome."

This meant that Titus Andronicus had been chosen to be a candidate for Roman Emperor.

Marcus Andronicus continued: "A nobler man, a braver warrior, does not live this day within the city walls. He is our General, and the Roman Senate has summoned him home from fighting weary wars against the barbarous Germanic people known as the Goths. With his sons, Titus Andronicus, a terror to our foes, has yoked a strong nation that has been trained up in weapons. He has made the Goths submit to Roman rule. Ten years have passed since he first undertook this cause of Rome and wielded weapons to chastise our enemies' pride. Five times he has returned bleeding to Rome, bearing his valiant sons in coffins from the battlefield, and now at last, laden with the spoils of honor, good Titus Andronicus returns to Rome — he is renowned and flourishing in arms.

"Let us entreat you, Saturninus and Bassianus, out of respect for the name of the late Emperor, the man whom you would like to now worthily succeed as Emperor, and out of respect for the rights of the Capitol and the Senate, rights that you profess to honor and adore, that you withdraw and abate your strength by disarming. Dismiss your followers and, as suitors should, plead your merits and make your case to be Emperor in peace and humbleness."

Saturninus said, "How civilly the Tribune speaks to calm my thoughts!"

Bassianus said, "Marcus Andronicus, I so trust in your uprightness and integrity, and I so love and honor you and yours, your noble brother Titus and his sons, and Titus' daughter, gracious Lavinia, who humbles all my thoughts and is Rome's rich ornament, that I will here dismiss my loving friends, and to my fortunes and the people's favor I will commit my cause in balance to be weighed."

The followers of Bassianus left.

Saturninus said, "Friends, who have been thus forward in supporting my right to be Emperor, I thank you all and here dismiss you all, and to the love and favor of my country I commit myself, my person, and my cause."

The followers of Saturninus left.

Saturninus added, "Rome, be as just and gracious to me as I am confident and kind to you."

He then said to the people in the Capital, "Open the gates, and let me in."

Bassianus added, "Tribunes, let me, a poor candidate, in."

The gates opened, and Saturninus and Bassianus went inside the Capitol.

A Captain arrived before the Capitol and said, "Romans, make way. Clear a path for the good Titus Andronicus, patron of virtue, Rome's best champion, successful in the battles that he fights. He has returned to Rome with honor and with fortune from the place where he rounded up the enemies of Rome with his sword and brought them to yoke."

Drums and trumpets sounded.

Martius and Mutius, two of Titus Andronicus' four remaining living sons, entered. Next came men carrying two coffins covered with black. Next came Titus Andronicus' two other living sons: Lucius and Quintus — Lucius was Titus' oldest living son. Next Titus Andronicus himself arrived. He was followed by Tamora, the Queen of the Goths, and by her sons: Alarbus, Demetrius, and Chiron. Tamora and her sons were Titus' prisoners. With them was Aaron, a Moor who was Tamora's lover. Some other Goths, who were also prisoners, followed, along with some Roman soldiers and Roman citizens.

The men carrying the coffins set them down.

Titus Andronicus said, "Hail, Rome, victorious in your mourning clothes! Just as the ship, which has discharged her freight, returns with precious new cargo to the bay from whence at first she weighed her anchors, here returns me, Andronicus, my temples bound with laurel boughs, to re-salute my country with his tears — tears of true joy for my return to Rome.

"Jupiter, King of the gods and great defender of this Capitol, show favor to the rites that we intend to observe!

"Romans, of my twenty-five valiant sons, half of the fifty sons that King Priam of Troy had, behold the poor remains, alive and dead! Here are two of my sons in coffins, and only four of my sons are left alive! Let Rome reward with love these sons of mine who still live. Let Rome reward with burial among their ancestors these of my sons whom I bring to their final home."

He paused and then said, "The Goths have given me leave to sheathe my sword."

Titus meant that by being conquered, the Goths had made it unnecessary for him to brandish his sword and fight them.

He then said, addressing himself, "Titus, you are unkind and negligent to your own dead. Why do you allow your sons, who are still unburied, to hover on the dreadful shore of the River Styx in the Underworld? Until your sons have been properly buried, their spirits cannot cross the River Styx and enter the Land of the Dead."

He ordered, "Make way so that I can lay them in the tomb by their brethren."

Some men opened the Tomb of the Andronici.

Titus Andronicus said, "Dead sons of mine, greet your ancestors in silence, as the dead are accustomed to be, and sleep in peace, you who were slain in your country's wars!

"Oh, sacred repository of my joys, sweet room of virtue and nobility, how many sons of mine you have inside you — sons whom you will never give to me again!"

Lucius, Titus' oldest living son, said to him, "Give us the proudest prisoner of the Goths so that we may cut off his limbs and on a pile of wood sacrifice his flesh *ad manes fratrum* — to the spirits of our brothers — in front of this earthy prison of their bones. That way, their spirits will not be unappeased and we will not be disturbed by unnatural happenings on Earth."

Titus Andronicus replied, "I give to you the noblest Goth who survives — the eldest son of this distressed Queen."

"Stop, Roman brethren — Roman religious observers!" Tamora, the Queen of the Goths, and a mother, said as she knelt. "Gracious conqueror, victorious Titus, pity the tears I am shedding. These are a mother's tears shed in great grief for her son. If your sons were ever dear to you, then think that my son is as dear to me! Isn't it enough that we have been brought to Rome, captive to you and to your Roman yoke, to appear in and beautify your triumphal procession at your return, but must my sons be slaughtered in the streets because of their valiant doings in their country's cause?

"If to fight for King and nation is piety in your sons, it is also piety in these boys — my sons. Andronicus, do not stain your tomb with blood. Do you want to emulate the nature of the gods? Then emulate them in being merciful. Sweet mercy is nobility's true badge. Thrice noble Titus, spare my first-born son."

"Be calm, madam, and pardon me," Titus Andronicus said. "These are their brethren, their brothers, whom you Goths beheld alive and dead, and for their slain brethren, they ask for a sacrifice as part of their religion. To be this sacrifice, your son has been selected, and he must die to appease the groaning spirits of those who are dead and gone."

"Away with him!" Lucius ordered. "Make a fire right away, and with our swords, upon a pile of wood, let's cut off his limbs and burn them until they are entirely consumed."

Titus Andronicus' four living sons — Lucius, Martius, Mutius, and Quintus — exited with Alarbus, Tamora's oldest son, as their prisoner.

"This is cruel, irreligious piety!" Tamora mourned as she stood up.

"Scythia is known for the barbarism of its inhabitants," Tamora's son Chiron said, "but have the Scythians ever been half as barbarous as these Romans?"

"Don't compare the Scythians to the ambitious Romans," Tamora's son Demetrius said. "Alarbus goes to his eternal rest, and we survive to tremble under Titus' threatening looks. Therefore, madam, accept that this sacrifice will happen, but hope as well that the same gods who gave Hecuba, the Queen of Troy, the opportunity to exact severe and merciless revenge upon the Thracian tyrant in his tent will favor Tamora, the Queen of the Goths — when Goths were Goths and Tamora was Queen — to avenge these bloody wrongs upon her foes."

The Thracian tyrant was Polymestor, to whom Hecuba's son Polydorus had been sent — with treasure — for his safety during the Trojan War. After Troy fell, King Polymestor of Thrace killed Polydorus so he could keep the treasure. The leader of the Greeks, Agamemnon, had fallen in love with Cassandra, one of Hecuba's daughters, and Hecuba was able to get Agamemnon to allow her and some other Trojan women to see Polymestor and his sons. The Trojan women killed Polymestor's sons, and Hecuba scratched out his eyes and blinded him, thus getting revenge for the death of her son Polydorus.

Titus Andronicus' four living sons — Lucius, Martius, Mutius, and Quintus — returned. Their swords were bloody.

Lucius said to his father, Titus, "See, lord and father, how we have performed our Roman rites. Alarbus' limbs have been cut off, and his entrails now feed the sacrificing fire, whose smoke, like incense, perfumes the sky. Nothing remains to be done except to inter our brethren in the tomb, and with loud trumpet calls welcome them to Rome."

Titus Andronicus replied, "Let it be done, and let Titus Andronicus make this his last farewell to their souls."

Trumpets sounded, and the two coffins were placed in the Tomb of the Andronici.

Titus said, "In peace and honor rest here, my sons. Rome's readiest champions, repose here in rest, secure from worldly chances and mishaps! Here lurks no treason, here no envy swells, here grow no damned grudges; here are no storms, no noise, but only silence and eternal sleep. In peace and honor rest here, my sons!"

Lavinia, Titus' daughter, arrived in time to hear the end of Titus' speech.

She said, "In peace and honor may Lord Titus live long. My noble lord and father, live on in fame! At this tomb my tears I render as tribute for my brethren's funeral obsequies, and at your feet I kneel, with tears of joy, shed on the earth, for your return to Rome. Oh, bless me here with your victorious hand, whose fortunes Rome's best citizens applaud!"

"Kind Rome, you have thus lovingly kept safe the comfort of my old age to gladden my heart! Lavinia, live; outlive your father's days, and as a reward for your virtue outlive even eternal fame!"

Marcus Andronicus and the Tribunes came out of the Capitol to greet Titus Andronicus. So did Saturninus and Bassianus.

Marcus Andronicus said, "Long live Lord Titus, my beloved brother, who is a gracious conquering general in the eyes of Rome!"

"Thanks, gentle Tribune, my noble brother Marcus," Titus replied.

"And welcome, nephews, home from successful wars," Marcus Andronicus said. "I mean you who survive, as well as you who sleep in fame! Fair lords who drew your swords in your country's service, your fortunes are alike. But the safer triumph belongs to those for whom we hold this funeral pomp because they have aspired to Solon's happiness and they have triumphed over chance by being in honor's bed — the grave!"

When Croesus, King of Lydia, asked the wise Athenian Solon who was happier than he, Croesus, Solon named three men, all of whom were dead. He then said, "Call no man happy until he is dead." By this, he meant that the goddess Fortune is fickle, and a man who is happy and fortunate today may be unhappy and unfortunate tomorrow.

Marcus continued, "Titus Andronicus, the people of Rome, whose friend in justice you have ever been, send to you by me, their Tribune and their trust, this robe of white and spotless hue, and they have nominated you as a candidate to be Emperor, as are these our late-deceased Emperor's sons. Therefore, be a candidate and put on this white robe and help to set a head on headless Rome."

"Rome's glorious body needs a better head than mine, which shakes because of old age and feebleness," Titus replied. "Why should I don this white robe, and trouble you? I might be chosen with proclamations today, but tomorrow yield up my rule and give up my life and die, and then all of you will have to redo all this business.

"Romans, I have been your soldier for forty years, and I have led my country's strength successfully and buried twenty-one valiant sons who were knighted on the battlefield, slain manfully while bearing weapons and performing rightful service for their noble country. Give me a staff of honor for my old age, but do not give me a scepter with which I can control the world. The man who held that scepter most recently, lords, wielded it justly."

Marcus Andronicus, who knew the will of the people, said, "Titus, if you ask to be Emperor, you will be elected."

Saturninus said, "Proud and ambitious Tribune, are you really quite sure of that?"

"Be calm, Prince Saturninus," Titus said.

Saturninus, who was not calm, said, "Romans, do right by me. Patricians, draw your swords and do not sheathe them until I, Saturninus, am Rome's Emperor.

"Titus Andronicus, I wish you would be shipped to Hell rather than rob me of the people's hearts!"

Lucius, who understood what his father, who respected old customs and values, wanted to do, said, "Proud Saturninus, you are interrupting the good thing that noble-minded Titus intends to do for you!"

Titus said, "Be calm, Prince Saturninus. I will restore to you the people's hearts, and I will have them elect you as Emperor although you are not their first choice."

Bassianus made a bid for Titus' support: "Andronicus, I do not flatter you, but I do honor you, and I will honor you until I die. I will be most thankful if you strengthen my faction — those who want me to be Emperor — with your friends. To men of noble minds, thanks are an honorable reward."

Titus did not change his mind about supporting Saturninus' candidacy to be Emperor: "People of Rome, and people's Tribunes here, I ask for your support and your votes: Will you bestow them in a friendly way and support whom Andronicus supports?"

The Tribunes replied, "To gratify the good Andronicus and to welcome his safe return to Rome, the people will accept as Emperor whomever he supports."

"Tribunes, I thank you," Titus said, "and I make a formal request that you elect your old Emperor's eldest son, Lord Saturninus, as Emperor. His virtues will, I hope, reflect on Rome the way that the Sun-god's rays reflect on Earth, and ripen justice and make it flourish in this commonwealth. Therefore, if you will elect to be Emperor the person whom I support, crown Saturninus and say, 'Long live our Emperor!'"

Romans shouted their approval, and Marcus Andronicus crowned Saturninus as Emperor.

Saturninus said, "Titus Andronicus, for your favors done to us in our election as Emperor this day, I give you thanks in partial payment of what you deserve from me, and I will with deeds reward your nobility and courtesy. And, for the first deed, Titus, I will advance your name and honorable family by making your daughter, Lavinia, my Empress, Rome's royal mistress, and mistress of my heart. In the sacred Pantheon, I will marry her. Tell me, Andronicus, does this proposal please you?"

Titus replied, "It does, my worthy lord; and in this match I regard myself to be highly honored by your grace. Here in sight of the Romans, I consecrate my sword, my chariot, and my prisoners to Saturninus. These presents are well worthy of Rome's imperial lord. Receive them; they are the tribute that I owe you. These are the symbols of my honor, and they lie humbled at your feet."

"Thanks, noble Titus, father of my life!" Saturninus said. "Rome shall record how proud I am of you and of your gifts, and when I forget the least of these indescribable rewards, Romans, forget your duty to be loyal to me."

Titus said to Tamora, "Now, madam, you are prisoner to an Emperor. He is a man who, because of your honor and your status, will treat you and your followers nobly."

Looking at Tamora closely for the first time, Saturninus thought, *Tamora is a beautiful lady, believe you me. She is of the hue and complexion that I would choose, were I to choose anew. If I had not already chosen to marry Lavinia, I would choose to marry Tamora.*

He said to Tamora, "Clear up, fair Queen, your cloudy countenance. Though the deeds of war have wrought this change in your countenance, you have not been brought to Rome to be made an object of mockery. You shall be treated like nobility in every way. Believe what I say, and do not let unhappiness daunt all your hopes. Madam, he who comforts you — and I am the one comforting you — can make you greater than the Queen of the Goths."

He then said to Lavinia, who of course had heard what he said to Tamora, "Lavinia, are you displeased by what I have said?"

"No, my lord," Lavinia replied, "I know that your true nobility has caused you to say these words with a Princely courtesy."

"Thanks, sweet Lavinia," Saturninus said. "Romans, let us go. Here we set our prisoners free without ransom."

He added, "Proclaim our honors, lords, with trumpets and drums."

As the trumpets and drums sounded, Saturninus spoke quietly to Tamora.

Bassianus, who was betrothed — engaged to marry — Lavinia, said, "Lord Titus, by your leave, this maiden is mine."

He put his arms around Lavinia.

Titus said to him, "What, sir! Are you in earnest then, my lord?"

"Yes, noble Titus," Bassianus replied, "and I am entirely resolved to do myself the right and reasonable course of action of marrying Lavinia."

"'*Suum cuique*' — 'to each his own' — is our Roman justice," Marcus Andronicus said. "This Prince is justly seizing nothing but what is already his own."

Lucius said, "And he will and shall have Lavinia if I, Lucius, live."

Titus Andronicus, who had just given permission to Saturninus to marry Lavinia, said, "Traitors, get away from here! Where is the Emperor's guard? Treason, my lord! Lavinia is ambushed and captured!"

"Captured!" Saturninus said. "By whom?"

Bassianus answered, "By him who justly may carry his betrothed away from all the world."

Bassianus, Marcus Andronicus, and Lavinia ran through a door.

Titus' son Mutius said, "Brothers, help to convey Lavinia away from here, and with my sword I'll guard this door and keep anyone from pursuing Lavinia."

Titus' sons Lucius, Martius, and Quintus ran through the door to help Lavinia run safely away.

Titus said to Saturninus, "My lord, continue to follow your plan to marry Lavinia. I'll soon bring her back."

He approached the door through which Saturninus and Lavinia had fled.

His son Mutius said, "My lord, you shall not pass through the door here."

"What, villain boy!" Titus said. "Do you bar my way anywhere in Rome?"

He stabbed his son.

Mutius cried, "Help, Lucius, help!"

Then he died.

During the fight, Saturninus, Tamora, Demetrius, Chiron, and Aaron went through a door and climbed up into the Capitol. They were able to look down and see Titus Andronicus.

Lucius came back, saw that Titus had killed Mutius, and said to his father, "My lord, you are unjust, and more than unjust, because you have slain your son without a just reason."

Titus replied, "Neither you, nor he, are any sons of mine. My sons would never so dishonor me as you have done. Traitor, restore Lavinia to the Emperor."

"I will restore her dead, if you wish," Lucius said, "but I will not give Lavinia to him to be his wife because she is another man's lawfully promised love."

He exited through the door.

Looking down on Titus, Emperor Saturninus said, "No, Titus, no; the Emperor does not need Lavinia. The Emperor does not need her, or you, or any of your stock. I'll trust, but only very slowly, a man after he mocks me once, but I will never trust you or your traitorous haughty sons — all of you worked together to dishonor me in this way. Was there no one else in Rome to make a laughingstock other than me? Very well, Andronicus, this deed is consistent with that proud brag of yours — you said that I begged you to make me Emperor."

Of course, this accusation was not true.

"Monstrous!" Titus said. "What reproachful words are these?"

"Go. Now. Leave here," Emperor Saturninus said. "Go and give that fickle woman to the man who drew his sword and flourished it in the air to win her. You shall enjoy a valiant son-in-law; he is fit to join with and fight beside your lawless sons in the commonwealth of Rome."

"These words are like razors to my wounded heart," Titus said.

Saturninus then proposed to Tamora: "And therefore, lovely Tamora, Queen of Goths, who like the stately Moon goddess Phoebe among her nymphs outshines the most splendid dames of Rome, if you should be pleased with this my sudden choice, behold, I choose you, Tamora, to be my bride, and I will make you Empress of Rome.

"Speak, Queen of Goths, do you applaud my choice? Will you marry me?

"I swear here by all the Roman gods, since priest and holy water are so near and candles burn so brightly and everything stands in readiness for Hymenaeus, the god of marriage, I will not walk the streets of Rome, or climb up to my palace, until from forth this place I lead my married bride beside me."

Kneeling, Tamora replied, "And here, in the sight of Heaven, to the Romans I swear that if Saturninus marries the Queen of Goths and makes her Empress, she will be a handmaid to his desires, and a loving nurse and mother to his youth."

"Arise, fair Queen, and let us go to the Pantheon to be married," Saturninus said. He ignored Titus as he said, "Lords, accompany your noble Emperor and his lovely bride, sent by the Heavens for Prince Saturninus; her wisdom in agreeing to marry me has conquered her misfortune. Go with us to the Pantheon, and there we shall perform our marriage rites."

Everyone except Titus departed.

Alone, Titus said to himself, "I am not invited to wait upon this bride. Titus, when were you ever accustomed to walk alone, dishonored like this, and accused of wrongs and crimes?"

Marcus Andronicus and Titus' three remaining living sons — Lucius, Martius, and Quintus — returned.

Marcus Andronicus said, "Titus, see, oh, see what you have done! You have killed a virtuous son in a bad quarrel. You did not have a good reason to kill him."

"No, foolish Tribune," Titus replied. "I have not killed unworthily any son of mine, and I have not killed you, or these sons of mine, who are confederates in the deed that has dishonored all our family. You are an unworthy brother, and these are unworthy sons!"

Lucius requested, "Allow us to give our brother burial, as is fitting. Allow us to give Mutius burial with our brethren."

"Traitors, go away!" Titus shouted. "He will not rest in this tomb. For five hundred years has stood this monument, which I have sumptuously re-built. Here none but soldiers and Rome's officers repose in fame; none basely slain in brawls are buried here. Bury him wherever you can; he will not be buried here."

Marcus said to Titus, "My lord, this is impiety in you. My nephew Mutius' honorable deeds plead for him. He must be buried with his brethren."

Quintus and Martius said, "And he shall, or we will accompany him in death."

Titus asked, "What villain was it who said, 'And he shall'?"

Quintus replied, "He who would maintain it in any place but here."

"What, would you bury him to spite me?" Titus asked.

"No, noble Titus," Marcus Andronicus said, "but I beg you to pardon Mutius and to bury him."

"Marcus, even you have metaphorically struck my helmet," Titus replied. "And, with these boys, you have wounded my honor. I consider every one of you to be my enemy, so trouble me no more, but get you gone."

Martius said, "He is not himself; let us withdraw."

Quintus said, "Not I — not until Mutius' bones have been buried."

Marcus Andronicus and Titus' three living sons kneeled before him.

Marcus Andronicus said, "Brother, for that is what you are to me —"

Quintus said, "Father, for that is what you are to me —"

Titus said, "Speak no more, if you know what is good for you."

Marcus said, "Renowned Titus, you are more than half my soul —"

Lucius said, "Dear father, you are the soul and substance of us all —"

Marcus pleaded, "Permit me, your brother, to inter my noble nephew here in the nest of virtue. Mutius died honorably as he helped Lavinia. You are Roman; do not be barbarous. The Greeks after careful consideration buried Great Ajax, who slew himself; wise Laertes' son, Ulysses, graciously pleaded for Great Ajax' funeral. Let not young Mutius, then, who was your joy, be barred his entrance here into the Tomb of the Andronici."

Great Ajax was the second strongest warrior of the Greeks during the Trojan War; Achilles was the first. After Achilles died, Achilles' mother, the sea goddess Thetis, wanted to award Achilles' magnificent armor, which had been made by the blacksmith god Vulcan, to one of the Greek warriors. Both Great Ajax and Ulysses argued that he should be awarded the armor, which was eventually given to Ulysses. Great Ajax went insane and killed some sheep, thinking that they were Ulysses and Agamemnon, who was the leader of the Greeks. When Great Ajax regained his sanity, he was so ashamed that he committed suicide. Ulysses convinced his fellow Greeks that Great Ajax should be given a proper funeral.

Marcus had pleaded well. He knew that Titus, his brother, would respond favorably to an ancient exemplum, especially one involving famous warriors.

Titus said, "Rise, Marcus, rise. This is the most dismal day that I have ever seen. On this day my sons dishonored me in Rome! Well, bury him, and next you shall bury me."

Marcus Andronicus and Titus' living sons placed Mutius in the Tomb of the Andronici. Great Ajax had died because he valued honor so much; Titus realized that Mutius, his son, had believed that he was protecting the honor of Lavinia, his sister, who was engaged to Saturninus.

Lucius said, "There your bones will lie, sweet Mutius, with your friends, until we adorn your tomb with memorial tokens."

All knelt and said, "Let no man shed tears for noble Mutius: He who died for the sake of virtue lives on in fame." Then they stood again.

"My lord, let us step out of these dreary dumps and this melancholy," Marcus said to Titus. "How came it to happen that the cunning Queen of Goths is so suddenly advanced in Rome? She has gone from being a captive to being the Roman Empress!"

"I don't know how it happened, Marcus," Titus replied, "but I know it did happen. Whether or not it happened as part of a plot, the Heavens can tell. Is she not then indebted to the man who brought her to such a height? Yes, and she will nobly remunerate him."

Saturninus and Tamora walked through one door. With them were Tamora's sons Demetrius and Chiron, and Aaron the Moor. Saturninus and Tamora were now married.

Bassianus, Lavinia, and some attendants walked through another door. Bassianus and Lavinia were now married.

Angry, Saturninus said, "So, Bassianus, you have won your bout." He added, sarcastically, "May God give you joy, sir, of your gallant bride!"

"And you of yours, my lord!" Bassianus said. "I have no more to say to you, nor do I wish any less for you; and so, I take my leave of you."

"Traitor, if Rome has law or we have power," Saturninus said, using the royal plural, "you and your faction shall repent this kidnapping of Lavinia."

"Do you call it kidnapping, my lord, when I seize what is my own — my truly betrothed love who is now my wife? But let the laws of Rome determine all; in the meanwhile I possess what is mine."

"Very well, sir," Saturninus said. "You are very short with us, but if we live, we'll be as sharp with you."

Bassianus replied, "My lord, what I have done, as best I may I must answer for it and shall do with my life. However, I want your grace to know this: By all the duties that I owe to Rome, this noble gentleman, Lord Titus here, has had his reputation and honor wronged. When I rescued Lavinia, Titus with his own hand slew his youngest son because of his zeal to serve you and because he was so highly moved to wrath when his desire to freely give Lavinia to you was balked. Return him, then, to your favor, Saturninus. Titus has shown in all his deeds that he is a father and a friend to you and Rome."

Titus Andronicus said, "Prince Bassianus, stop pleading for me and my deeds. It is you and those who helped you who have dishonored me."

He knelt and said, "May Rome and the righteous Heavens be my judge for how I have loved and honored Saturninus!"

Tamora said to Saturninus, her husband, "My worthy lord, if ever Tamora were gracious in those Princely eyes of yours, then hear me speak impartially for all, and at my request, sweetheart, pardon what is past."

Saturninus replied, "What, madam! Shall I be dishonored openly, and basely put my sword in its sheath without getting revenge?"

Tamora said, "No, my lord; may the gods of Rome forbid that I should be a person who causes you to be dishonored! But on my honor I vouch for good Lord Titus' innocence in everything; his fury — which is not faked — shows that his grievances are real. Therefore, at my request, look graciously on him. Do not lose so noble a friend on an idle supposition, and do not afflict his gentle heart with sour looks."

She then said quietly to Saturninus so that others could not hear, "My lord, do as I advise you. Be won over at last. Hide all your feelings of grief and discontent. You are only newly planted in your throne. Be afraid, then, that the common people — and the patricians, too — after justly considering the situation, will take Titus' part and replace you as Emperor because you are showing ingratitude, which Rome considers to be a heinous sin. Yield to my entreaty; and then leave it to me. I'll find a day to massacre them all and raze their faction and their family, the cruel father and his traitorous sons, to whom I begged for my dear son's life, and I will make them know what it is to let a Queen kneel in the streets and beg for mercy in vain."

She said out loud so all could hear, "Come, come, sweet Emperor; come, Titus Andronicus. Emperor, tell this good old man to stand up, and cheer up Titus' heart that now dies in the tempest of your angry frown."

"Rise, Titus, rise," Saturninus said. "My Empress has prevailed over me."

"I thank your Majesty, and her, my lord," Titus said, standing up. "These words, these looks, infuse new life in me."

"Titus, I am now a part of Rome," Tamora said. "I am now a happily adopted and naturalized Roman, and I must advise the Emperor for his good. This day all quarrels die, Andronicus. Let it be to my honor, my good lord, that I have reconciled your friends and you. As for you, Prince Bassianus, I have given my word and promise to the Emperor that you will be more mild and obedient. Do not be afraid, my lords, and you, Lavinia. Take my advice, all of you, and humble yourselves by getting on your knees and asking for a pardon from his Majesty."

Marcus, Lavinia, and Titus' three remaining living sons knelt.

Lucius said, "We kneel, and we vow to Heaven and to his Highness that what we did was done as mildly as we could, considering the situation — we protected our sister's honor and our own."

Marcus said, "On my honor, I say that this is true."

Saturninus said, "Go away now, and talk no more; trouble us no more."

"No, no, sweet Emperor, we must all be friends," Tamora said. "Marcus the Tribune and his nephews kneel and ask for your grace. I will not be denied: Sweetheart, look at them."

Saturninus said, "Marcus, for your sake and your brother Titus' here, and at my lovely Tamora's entreaty, I pardon these young men's heinous faults. All of you, stand up."

They stood up.

Saturninus continued, "Lavinia, although you left me as if I were a churl — a peasant — I found a sweetheart, and as sure as death I swore I would not part from the priest as a bachelor. If the Emperor's court can feast two brides, you are my guest, Lavinia, and so are your friends.

"This day shall be a love-day, Tamora. On this day, I shall forgive faults and resolve disputes."

Titus Andronicus said, "Tomorrow, if it will please your Majesty to hunt the panther and the male deer with me, with horns and hounds we'll give your grace *bonjour* — a good day."

Saturninus replied, "So be it, Titus, and gramercy — great thanks — too."

CHAPTER 2

— 2.1 —

In front of the palace, Aaron the Moor stood alone.

He said to himself, "Now Tamora has climbed to the top of Mount Olympus, home of the gods. She is safe from the slings and arrows of Lady Fortune, and she sits aloft, on high, safe from the crack of thunder and the flash of lightning. She has advanced so high that she is above the threatening reach of pale and envious people.

"Tamora now is just like the golden Sun that salutes the morning and after having gilded the ocean with its yellow beams gallops through the zodiac in its glistening coach, and looks over the highest hills. Upon her does Earthly honor wait, and virtue stoops and trembles at her frown.

"So, then, Aaron, arm your heart and fit your thoughts to mount aloft with your imperial mistress, and mount with her as high as she goes, whom you in triumph have long held prisoner, fettered in amorous chains and faster bound to Aaron's eyes that bewitch and charm than Prometheus is tied to a rock in the Caucasus, a mountain range in Caucasia."

Aaron had been having an affair with Tamora and so he had mounted her, and he intended to benefit from her rise in fortune. She was bound by love to him as securely as Prometheus, who had stolen fire from the gods to give to human beings, was chained to a rock in the Caucasus — as Prometheus' punishment for helping human beings, Zeus had chained him to that rock. Each day, an eagle ate Prometheus' liver, which grew back each day and was eaten again the following day.

Aaron continued, "Away with slavish clothing and servile thoughts! I will be bright and shine in pearl and gold as I serve this newly made Empress. To serve, did I say? I mean to wanton sexually with this Queen, this goddess, this Semiramis, this nymph, this Siren, who will charm Rome's Saturninus, and see the shipwreck of himself and his commonwealth."

Aaron compared Tamora to Semiramis, an Assyrian Queen who was known for her power, sexual appetite, cruelty, and beauty.

He also compared her to a Siren, who would sing beautifully in order to cause sailors to become entranced by her song and wreck their ships on the shore of her island.

Aaron, hearing some people fighting, said, "Hello! What storm is this?"

Tamora's two living sons — Demetrius and Chiron — came near Aaron. They were shouting and swaggering.

Demetrius said, "Chiron, you are not as intelligent as your age suggests, and your intelligence cannot be sharp since you intrude where I am welcomed and may, for all you know, be loved."

Chiron replied, "Demetrius, you presume too much in everything, just like you are doing now as you try to intimidate me with your boasts. You are older than I am by only a year or two, and that is not enough to make me less gracious than you or to make you more fortunate than me. I am as able and as fit as you are to serve and to deserve my mistress' favor. I shall use my sword to prove that to you, and I shall use it to plead my passion for Lavinia and her love."

Aaron said quietly to himself, "Clubs! Clubs! These lovers will not keep the peace."

The phrase "Clubs! Clubs!" was a call to the city watch to come and use their clubs to break up a fight in the city streets — or a call to apprentices to grab clubs and come and fight on one or the other side.

Demetrius said, "Why, boy, although our mother, unwisely, gave you a dancing-rapier — used for fashion and decoration while dancing, and not used for fighting — to wear by your side, have you grown so desperate that you threaten your friends? Ha! Have your useless sword — a stage prop! — glued inside your sheath until you know better how to handle it."

Chiron replied, "Meanwhile, sir, you shall perceive very well how much I dare to do with the little skill I have."

Addressing him by an insulting title, Demetrius said, "Boy, have you grown that brave?"

They drew their swords.

Having naked weapons so near the palace was illegal, and could result in serious punishment, including death, and so Aaron now intervened.

He came forward and said, "Why, what is going on now, lords! Do you dare to draw your swords so near the Emperor's palace and engage in such a quarrel openly? I know very well the reason for all this quarreling. I would not for a million gold pieces allow that reason to be learned by them it most concerns, and your mother — even for much more than a million gold pieces — would not allow herself to be so dishonored in the court of Rome as that would make her. For shame, put up your swords."

Demetrius said, "Not I, not until I have sheathed my rapier in his bosom and completely thrust down his throat these reproachful speeches that he has breathed to my dishonor here."

"I am prepared and fully resolved to fight you," Chiron said. "You are a foul-spoken coward, who thunders with your tongue, but who dares to do nothing with your weapon!"

"Put your swords away, I say!" Aaron thundered. "Now, by the gods that warlike Goths adore, this petty quarrel will ruin us all. Why, lords, aren't you thinking how dangerous it is to encroach upon a Prince's right? Lavinia is married to Prince Bassianus. Has Lavinia then become so loose, or Bassianus so degenerate, that for her love such quarrels may be raised without check, justice, or revenge? Young lords, beware! If the Empress should learn the reason for this discord, the music would not please her."

"I don't care whether she and all the world know," Chiron said. "I love Lavinia more than all the world."

Demetrius said, "Youngster, learn to choose to love someone of a lower social status. Lavinia is your elder brother's desired."

"What! Are you mad?" Aaron asked. "Don't you know how furious and impatient men can be? Don't you know that they cannot tolerate competitors in love? I tell you, lords, you are pursuing your own deaths when you pursue Lavinia in this way."

"Aaron, I would be ready to meet a thousand deaths in order to achieve her whom I love," Chiron replied.

"To achieve her!" Aaron said. "What do you mean?"

"Why are you pretending not to understand?" Demetrius asked. "She is a woman, and therefore may be wooed. She is a woman, and therefore may be won. She is Lavinia, and therefore must be loved. Why, man, more water glides by the mill than the miller knows of; and we all know it is easy to steal a slice from a cut loaf of bread. Why can't we steal a piece of ass? Although Bassianus is the Emperor's brother, better than he have worn Vulcan's badge."

Vulcan's badge was the horns of a cuckold — a man whose wife had cheated on him. Vulcan, the blacksmith god, was married to Venus, who had an affair with Mars, the war god.

Aaron thought, *Someone as high ranking as Saturninus may wear Vulcan's badge.*

Demetrius continued, "Then why should a man despair who knows to court a woman with the help of words, fair looks, and liberality? Haven't you very often struck a doe, and carried her by the gamekeeper's nose without getting caught?"

"Why, then, it seems, some certain snatch or so would serve your turns," Aaron said.

He meant that Demetrius and Chiron could snatch — kidnap — Lavinia and forcibly make her serve them sexually. In other words, Demetrius and Chiron could take turns raping her.

"Yes, so the turn were served," Chiron said. He wanted to make sure that he had his turn.

"Aaron, you have hit it — you have hit on the solution to our problem," Demetrius said.

"I wish that you had already hit it — by shooting your arrow into the center of your target," Aaron said. "Then we should not be troubled with this business. Why, listen! Are you two such fools that you would you argue over this solution to your problem? Would it offend you, then, if both of you would have sex with Lavinia?"

"Truly, that would not bother me," Chiron said.

"Nor me, so long as I had my turn with her," Demetrius said.

"For shame, be friends, and join together so that you can both get what you are fighting for," Aaron said. "Plots and stratagems must get you what you want; therefore, you must resolve that since you cannot achieve what you want the way you want to achieve it — that is, with words — you must therefore achieve it by what works — that is, with force.

"Learn this from me: Lucrece was not more chaste than this Lavinia, Bassianus' love."

Lucrece was an ancient Roman gentlewoman who committed suicide after being raped.

One meaning of chastity is abstinence from sex, but the meaning of chastity used here was abstinence from illicit sex, including extramarital sex.

Aaron continued, "A speedier course than lingering languishment you must pursue, and I have found the path. My lords, a ceremonious hunt will take place today. There the lovely Roman ladies will troop. The forest paths are wide and spacious, and many unfrequented places in the forest are suitable for rape and villainy. Separate this dainty doe from the rest of the herd in such a place and strike her home — have sex with her — by force, since words will not get you what you want. This is the only way you will have sex with Lavinia.

"Come, come, we will tell our Empress, Tamora, who has consecrated her wit and intelligence to villainy and vengeance, as if they were her religion, everything that we intend to do. She will sharpen our plot with advice and make it better. She will not allow you to fight each other, but she will help you get everything you wish.

"The Emperor's court is like the house of rumor and gossip. The palace is full of tongues, eyes, and ears. In contrast, the woods are ruthless and pitiless, dreadful, deaf, and dull. There speak, and strike, daring boys, and take your turns with Lavinia. There satisfy your lust, hidden from the eye of Heaven, and revel deep in Lavinia's treasury."

"Your counsel, lad, smells of no cowardice," Chiron said to Aaron.

Demetrius said, "*Sit fas aut nefas*, until I find the stream that will cool this heat I feel, a charm to calm these fits, *per Styga, per manes vehor*."

Sit fas aut nefas is Latin for "Whether right or wrong." *Per Styga, per manes vehor* is Latin for "I am borne through the Stygian realms." The Styx is a river in Hell, and so Demetrius was saying, "I am in Hell."

Considering the way that Demetrius was planning to treat Lavinia, whom he — and Chiron — had said they loved, he — and Chiron — deserved to be in Hell.

— **2.2** —

Titus Andronicus and his sons Lucius, Martius, and Quintus were in a forest near Rome. Also present were Marcus Andronicus and some hunters, hunting hounds, and attendants.

Titus Andronicus said, "The hunt is afoot. The early morning is bright and grey, the fields are fragrant, and the woods are green. Release the hunting hounds, and let them bay and awaken the Emperor Saturninus and his lovely bride and rouse Prince Bassianus. Also let the horns sound a hunter's peal so that all the court may echo with the noise.

"Sons, let it be your responsibility, as it is ours, to attend the Emperor's person carefully. I was troubled in my sleep last night, but this dawning day has inspired new comfort."

Hounds bayed and horns sounded. Saturninus and Tamora arrived, as did Bassianus and Lavinia. Demetrius and Chiron then arrived, along with some attendants.

Titus Andronicus said, "I give many good mornings to your Majesty. Madam, to you I give as many and as good. I promised your grace a hunter's peal."

"And you have rung it lustily, my lord," Saturninus said, "but somewhat too early for newly married ladies."

Bassianus asked, "Lavinia, what do you say to that?"

"I say that it is incorrect," Lavinia said. "I have been wide awake two hours and more."

"Come on, then," Saturninus said. "Let us have horses and chariots, and let us begin our hunt."

He said to Tamora, "Madam, now you shall see our Roman hunting."

"I have dogs, my lord," Marcus Andronicus said, "that will rouse the proudest panther in the hunting ground, and climb the top of the highest hill."

Titus Andronicus said, "And I have horses that will follow where the game makes its way and runs like swallows over the plain."

Demetrius said quietly to his brother, "Chiron, we will not hunt with horse or hound, but we hope to pluck a dainty doe from the crowd and throw her to the ground."

— 2.3 —

In a lonely part of the forest, Aaron, holding a bag of gold, stood by an elder tree.

He said to himself, "A man who has intelligence would think that I had none because I am burying so much gold under a tree and never afterward will possess it. Let him who thinks so badly of me know that this gold will coin a plot, which, cunningly effected, will beget a very excellent piece of villainy."

He buried the gold under the tree and said, "And so repose, sweet gold, for the unrest of those who receive alms out of the Empress' chest."

The "alms" were the gold that he had taken from the treasure chest of Tamora, who was now the Roman Empress.

Tamora entered the scene and said, "My lovely Aaron, why do you look solemn and serious, when everything is making a gleeful display? The birds chant melody on every bush, the snake lies coiled in the cheerful Sun, and the green leaves quiver with the cooling wind and make a checkered shadow on the ground. Under their sweet shade, Aaron, let us sit, and, while the babbling echo mocks the hounds' cries and replies shrilly to the well-tuned horns, as if a double hunt were heard at the same time, let us sit down and listen to their yelping noise, and after such 'conflict' such as the wandering Prince and Dido are supposed to have once enjoyed, when a happy and fortuitous storm surprised them and they then curtained themselves within a secret-keeping cave, we may, each of us wreathed in the other's arms, our pastimes done, enjoy a golden slumber while hounds and horns and sweet melodious birds be to us as is a wet nurse's song of lullaby to bring her babe sleep."

The wandering Prince was Aeneas, the Trojan warrior who survived the Fall of Troy and who was destined to go to Italy and become an important ancestor of the Roman people. Before he settled in Italy, a storm blew his ships and him to Carthage. Hoping to keep Aeneas from fulfilling his destiny, the goddess Juno created the right conditions for Aeneas and Dido, the Queen of Carthage, to have a love affair. During a hunt, a storm arose, and Aeneas and Dido sought shelter in a cave, where they made love for the first time.

Aaron replied, "Madam, although Venus governs your desires, Saturn is the planet that is the astrological dominator over my desires. What signifies my death-dealing eye, my silence and my cloudy melancholy, my fleece of woolly hair that now uncurls even as an adder does when she uncoils in order to perform some fatal execution? No, madam, these are not signs of sexual desire. Vengeance is in my heart, death is in my hand, and blood and revenge are hammering in my head.

"Listen, Tamora, the Empress of my soul, which never hopes to have more Heaven than rests in you. This is the day of doom for Bassianus. He will die today, and his Philomela will lose her tongue today. Your sons will make pillage of her chastity, and they will wash their hands in Bassianus' blood."

Philomela was an Athenian Princess who was raped by her sister's husband, Tereus, who cut out her tongue so that she could not tell anyone that he had raped her. Philomela wove a tapestry, however, that revealed the rape and rapist.

Aaron asked, "Do you see this letter?"

He handed it to Tamora and said, "Take this letter, which is written in a scroll and is integral to a deadly plot. Please give the letter to the King."

He saw Bassianus and Lavinia coming toward them and said, "Now ask me no more questions; we are seen. Here comes a part of the booty we hope for. They do not yet fear the destruction of their lives."

Tamora said, "Ah, my sweet Moor, you are sweeter to me than life!"

"No more, great Empress; Bassianus is coming. Be angry with him; and I'll go and fetch your sons to back you up in your quarrels, whatever they are."

Aaron exited.

Bassianus said to Tamora, "Who have we here? Rome's royal Empress, unaccompanied by her appropriate escorts? Or is it the goddess Diana, clothed like Tamora? Has Diana abandoned her holy groves to see the many people hunting in this forest?"

Bassianus was being gallant in comparing Tamora to Diana because goddesses are more beautiful than any mortal woman could ever be.

The choice of Diana to compare Tamora to was, however, ironic. Tamora was cuckolding her husband, while Diana was fiercely protective of her virginity. In fact, while hunting with his hounds the Theban Actaeon unintentionally saw Diana bathing naked in a pool of water. Diana turned him into a stag with a human mind, and then his hunting hounds picked up his scent and ripped him to pieces.

As Aaron had advised, Tamora picked a quarrel with Bassianus: "Saucy critic of our private steps! Had I the power that some say Diana had, your temples should be planted presently with horns, as were Actaeon's temples; and the hounds would fall upon your newly transformed limbs, unmannerly intruder as you are!"

Lavinia was angry and said, "By your leave, noble Empress, it is thought that you have an excellent gift for giving men horns."

She was referring to the horns of a cuckold; an unfaithful wife was said to give her husband horns.

Lavinia continued, "It is also suspected that your Moor and you have separated yourselves from the others so that you can try sexual experiments. May Jove, King of the gods, shield your husband from his hounds today! It would be a pity if they should mistake him for a stag."

Referring to Aaron the Moor, Bassianus said, "Believe me, Queen, your swarthy Cimmerian — a dark person who dwells in darkness — makes your honor his body's hue: stained, detested, and abominable. Why are you separated from all your train of followers, and why have you dismounted from your snow-white, good-looking steed and wandered here to an obscure plot of land, accompanied by only a barbarous Moor, if not because of your foul desire?"

Lavinia added, "Your being intercepted in your sport with the Moor is a great reason for you to berate my noble lord for what you call saucy and insolent rudeness."

She said to her husband, "Please, let us go away from here and let her enjoy her raven-colored love. This valley fits that purpose surpassingly well."

Bassianus said to Tamora, "The King my brother shall hear about this."

Lavinia added, "Yes, for these sexual slips of yours have long disgraced him. He is too good a King to be so mightily abused!"

Tamora said, "Why, I have patience to endure all this."

She had seen her sons, Demetrius and Chiron, coming, and she knew that she would soon get revenge for what they had said to her.

Demetrius said to her, "How are you, dear sovereign, and our gracious mother! Why does your Highness look so pale and wan?"

Tamora replied, "Don't I have reason to look pale? These two — Bassianus and Lavinia — have enticed me here to this place: You see that it is a barren and detested valley. The trees, although it is summer, are yet forlorn and lean, overcome with moss and baleful, parasitic mistletoe. Here the Sun never shines; here nothing breeds, except for the night-haunting owl or the ominous raven. And when they showed me this abhorrent pit, they told me that here, at the dead of night, a thousand fiends, a thousand hissing snakes, ten thousand poisonous toads that cause swelling, and as many goblins would make such fearful and confused cries that any mortal body hearing the sounds would immediately become insane, or else die suddenly.

"No sooner had they told this Hellish tale than immediately they told me they would tie me here to the body of a dismal yew tree, and leave me to this miserable death. And then they called me a foul adulteress, a lascivious Goth, and all the bitterest terms that any ear ever heard to such effect, and, if you had not by wondrous fortune come, they would have executed this vengeance on me.

"Revenge it, as you love your mother's life, or henceforth you will not be called my children."

Demetrius said to Tamora as he stabbed Bassianus with a dagger, "This is a witness that I am your son."

Chiron took the dagger from Demetrius, stabbed Bassianus, and said, "And this is a witness for me, struck home to show my strength."

Bassianus died.

Lavinia said to Tamora, "Yes, come, Semiramis — no, I should say barbarous Tamora, for no name fits your evil nature but your own!"

Semiramis was an Assyrian Queen who was known for her power, sexual appetite, cruelty, and beauty. Lavinia was insulting Tamora by saying that Semiramis' name was not associated with enough evil to be suitable as a name for Tamora.

Tamora said to Chiron, "Give me your dagger. My boys, you shall witness and know that your mother's hand shall right your mother's wrong."

"Stop, madam," Demetrius said. "More belongs to Lavinia than her life. First thresh the corn, and afterward burn the straw. This hussy made an issue of her chastity, her nuptial vow, and her loyalty to her husband, and with that false and old-fashioned pride confronted and insulted your mightiness. Shall she carry her chastity into her grave?"

"If she does, then I wish that I were a eunuch," Chiron said. "Let us drag her husband away from here to some secret hole, and make his dead trunk a pillow to our lust."

Tamora said, "But when you have the honey you desire, do not let this wasp survive and sting both of you two and me."

"I promise you, madam," Chiron said, "that we will make sure that she can do us no harm."

He said to Lavinia, "Come, mistress, now by force we will enjoy that nicely preserved chastity of yours."

Lavinia began to beg: "Oh, Tamora! You have the face of a woman —"

"I will not hear her speak," Tamora said to her sons. "Away with her!"

"Sweet lords, entreat her to listen to only a word from me," Lavinia begged Demetrius and Chiron.

"Listen, fair madam," Demetrius said to his mother, "let it be your glory to see her tears; but let your heart be to them as unrelenting and hard flint is to drops of rain."

"When did the tiger's young ones teach the mother?" Lavinia said to Demetrius. "Oh, do not teach her wrath; she taught wrath to you. The milk you sucked from her breasts turned to marble. Even as you sucked at her teats you learned your tyranny. Yet not every mother breeds identical sons."

Knowing that Demetrius would not help her, Lavinia turned to Chiron and begged, "Entreat her to show pity to a woman."

"What, would you have me prove myself a bastard?" Chiron replied.

"It is true; the raven does not hatch a lark," Lavinia said to him. "Yet I have heard — I wish I could find it to be true now! — that the lion, moved by pity, endured having his princely paws pared all away. Some say that ravens foster forlorn children, while their own young birds stay famished in their nests. Be to me, although your hard heart say no, not nearly as kind as the lion or the raven, but show me at least some pity!"

Lavinia had referred to a fable by Aesop in which a lion fell in love with a woman and agreed to have its claws pared and its teeth pulled so that her human relatives would not be afraid of it. Once these things were done, however, the woman's relatives drove away the defenseless lion.

She had also referred to a folktale in which a raven fed lost human children. In her version of the folktale, the raven's nestlings went hungry.

Neither story was likely to be effective with Tamora and her two sons, especially since Lavinia had, in her fear, mistakenly referred to paring the lion's paws instead of claws. Both stories also had bad consequences: The lion did not get his love, and the raven's own nestlings went hungry.

"I don't know what it means!" Tamora said. "Away with her!"

"Oh, let me teach you what I mean!" Lavinia said. "Let me teach you for my father's sake, who allowed you to live, when he might well have slain you. Be not obdurate — open your deaf ears."

"Had you personally never offended me," Tamora said, "I would be pitiless for his sake."

She said to her sons, "Remember, boys, I poured forth tears in vain to save your oldest brother, Alarbus, from the sacrifice, but fierce Titus Andronicus would not relent. Therefore, away with her, and use and treat her as you will. The worse you treat her, the better I love you."

"Oh, Tamora," Lavinia begged, "be called a gentle Queen, and with your own hands kill me in this place! For I have not begged so long for my life. I — poor me — was slain when Bassianus died."

She knelt and hugged Tamora's knees.

"What are you begging for, then?" Tamora asked. "Foolish woman, let me go."

"I beg for immediate death," Lavinia said. "And I beg for one thing more that womanhood will not allow my tongue to tell."

Lavinia was begging not to be raped, but she did not want to say the word "rape." She wanted Tamora to pity her and not allow her to be raped.

She begged Tamora, "Oh, keep me from their worse-than-killing lust and tumble me into some loathsome pit, where no man's eye may ever behold my body. Do this, and be a charitable murderer."

In her fear, Lavinia chose words badly. To tumble a woman meant to have sex with a woman.

"If I would do that, I would rob my sweet sons of their fee," Tamora said. "They hunted you and so they are entitled to a taste of you. I say no to your request; instead, I will let my sons satisfy their lust on you."

Falcons were fleshed after a successful hunt: They were given a taste of the flesh they had hunted.

"Let's go!" Demetrius said. "Lavinia, you have kept us here too long."

Lavinia said to Tamora, "No grace? No womanhood? Ah, beastly creature! You are a blot and enemy to the name of woman! May ruin fall —"

She had been about to curse Tamora by saying, "May ruin fall upon you," but Chiron covered her mouth with his hand and said, "You will say no more, for I have stopped your mouth."

He said to Demetrius, "Bring the body of her husband. This is the hole where Aaron told us to hide it."

Demetrius threw the body of Bassianus into the pit, and then he and Chiron dragged Lavinia away.

Alone, Tamora said to herself, "Farewell, my sons. Make sure that Lavinia can do no harm to us. May my heart never be merry again until all the Andronici are done away with and killed. Now I will go from here to seek my lovely Moor, and let my passionate sons deflower this whore."

She exited.

Aaron arrived. With him were Titus Andronicus' two younger sons: Martius and Quintus.

Aaron said, "Come on, my lords, put the better foot forward — hurry. Straightaway I will bring you to the loathsome pit where I saw the panther fast asleep."

"My sight is very dim," Quintus said. "It may forebode something bad."

"My sight is also very dim, I promise you," Martius said. "If it were not that I would be ashamed, I would be willing to leave the hunting and sleep awhile."

Aaron had covered the opening to the pit with vegetation. He maneuvered Martius so that Martius fell into the pit.

Quintus asked, "What have you fallen into? What treacherous and disguised hole is this, whose mouth is covered with wild, uncultivated briers, upon whose leaves are drops of newly shed blood as fresh as morning dew trickling down flowers? This is a very deadly place, I think. Speak, brother, have you hurt yourself in the fall?"

"Brother, I am hurt by the sight of the most dismal spectacle that ever a seeing eye has made a heart lament!"

Aaron thought, *Now I will fetch the King to find Martius and Quintus here, so that he will very likely think that these were the men who murdered his brother.*

He exited to find Emperor Saturninus.

Martius said, "Why don't you assist me, and help me out of this unholy and wicked and bloodstained hole?"

"I am bewildered by a strange fear," Quintus replied. "A chilling sweat overruns my trembling joints. My heart suspects more than my eye can see."

"To prove that you have a prophetic heart that is capable of discerning the truth, Aaron and you can look down into this den and see a fearful sight of blood and death."

Quintus looked around for Aaron, but he did not see him. He said, "Aaron is gone, and my compassionate heart will not permit my eyes once to behold the thing it imagines and trembles at. Tell me what it is, for never until now was I a child who feared something I did not know."

Martius replied, "Lord Bassianus lies soaked in blood here, prostate, like a slaughtered lamb in this detested, dark, blood-drinking pit."

"If it is dark, how do you know it is he?"

"Upon his bloody finger he wears a precious ring with a jewel that lightens all the hole. Like a candle in some tomb, it shines upon the dead man's pale cheeks, and shows the harsh interior of the pit. So pale did shine the Moon on Pyramus when he by night lay bathed in his virgin blood."

Pyramus loved Thisbe, and he arranged to meet her at night. Thisbe arrived first, and saw a lion. She ran away, leaving her mantle — her shawl — behind her, which the lion mauled. Pyramus arrived and found the mantle. He thought that a lion had killed Thisbe, and so he committed suicide.

Martius continued, "Oh, brother, help me with your fainting hand — if fear has made you faint, as it has me — out of this deadly devouring repository that is as hateful as the misty mouth of Cocytus, one of the rivers of Hell."

"Reach your hand out to me, so that I may help you out," Quintus said. "Or, if I lack the strength to do you so much good, reach your hand out to me so that I may be pulled into the swallowing womb of this deep pit, poor Bassianus' grave."

He pulled Martius' hand, let loose of it, and said, "I have no strength to pull you to the brink."

"And I have no strength to climb without your help."

"Give me your hand once more; I will not let loose again until you are here aloft with me, or I am below with you."

He pulled Martius' hand, and then he said, "You cannot come to me, and so I come to you."

He fell into the pit.

Aaron and Emperor Saturninus saw Quintus fall into the pit.

"Come along with me," Saturninus said, walking over to the pit. "I'll see what hole is here, and who he is who just now has leaped into it."

He then called into the pit, "Say who you are who just now descended into this gaping hollow of the earth."

From the pit, Martius replied, "I am the unhappy son of old Titus Andronicus. I came here in a most unlucky hour, and I found your brother, Bassianus, dead."

"My brother dead!" Saturninus said. "I know that you are only joking. He and his lady are both at the lodge upon the north side of this pleasant hunting ground. It is not an hour since I left him there."

Martius said, "We don't know where you left him alive, but — I hate to say this — here we have found him dead."

Tamora arrived with her attendants. Also accompanying her were Titus Andronicus and Lucius, his oldest son.

"Where is my lord the King?" Tamora asked.

"Here I am, Tamora, although I am wounded with killing grief."

"Where is Bassianus, your brother?"

"Now you are probing my wound to the bottom. Poor Bassianus lies here murdered."

"Then all too late I bring this deadly document," Tamora said. "It reveals the plot of this untimely tragedy, and I wonder greatly that a man's face can hide such murderous tyranny in the wrinkles of pleasing smiles."

She gave Saturninus the letter that Aaron had given to her.

Saturninus read the letter out loud: "*If we do not meet him at a convenient time and place — sweet huntsman, it is Bassianus we mean — dig his grave for him. You know what we mean. Look for your reward among the nettles at the elder tree that shades the mouth of the pit where we decided to bury Bassianus. Do this, and make us your lasting friends.*"

He said, "Oh, Tamora! Have you ever heard anything like this? This is the pit, and this is the elder tree. Look around, sirs, and see if you can find the huntsman who murdered Bassianus."

Aaron dug under the elder tree and said, "My gracious lord, here is the bag of gold."

Saturninus said to Titus Andronicus, "Two of your whelps, cruel curs of bloody character, have here bereft my brother of his life."

He ordered, "Sirs, drag them from the pit and take them to the prison. There let them stay until we have devised some never-heard-of torturing pain for them."

"What, are they in this pit?" Tamora said. "Oh, what a wondrous thing! How easily murder is exposed!"

Some attendants got Martius and Quintus out of the pit.

Titus Andronicus knelt and said, "High Emperor, upon my feeble knee I beg this boon, with tears not lightly shed, that this fell fault of my accursed sons — they are accursed if it is proved that they have committed this fell fault —"

"*If* it is proved!" Saturninus said. "You can see that it is obvious that they committed the murder."

He asked, "Who found this letter? Tamora, was it you?"

She replied, "Titus Andronicus himself found it and picked it up."

She had changed Aaron's plan.

"I did pick up the letter, my lord," Titus said, "yet let me be my two sons' bail. By my father's sacred tomb, I vow that they shall be ready at your Highness' will to answer what they are suspected of even with their lives."

"You shall not bail them," Saturninus said. "See that you follow me."

Titus Andronicus stood up.

Saturninus ordered, "Some of you bring the murdered body, and some of you bring the murderers. Let them not speak a word; their guilt is plain. By my soul, I say that if something was worse than death, it would be done to them."

As Saturninus exited, Tamora said, "Titus Andronicus, I will entreat the King for mercy. Fear not for your sons; they shall do well enough."

She exited.

Titus Andronicus said, "Come, Lucius, come; don't stay and try to talk to your brothers or their guards."

— 2.4 —

In another part of the forest, Demetrius and Chiron were taunting Lavinia, whom they had raped. They had also cut off her hands at the elbows and cut out her tongue so that she could not reveal who had raped and mutilated her.

Demetrius said to her, "So, now go and tell people, if your tongue can speak, who it was who cut out your tongue and raped you."

Chiron said to her, "Write down your mind and in that way reveal what you want to communicate, if your stumps will let you be an author."

Lavinia was flailing about.

Demetrius said, "Look at how she can communicate with signs and gestures."

"Go home, call for perfumed water, and wash your hands," Chiron said.

"She has no tongue to call for water, nor hands to wash, and so let's leave her to her silent walks," Demetrius said.

"If I were her, I would go hang myself," Chiron said.

"If you had hands to help you tie the noose," Demetrius said.

Demetrius and Chiron left Lavinia alone in the forest.

Marcus Andronicus, who was hunting, rode up on a horse, and saw Lavinia, who, ashamed, ran from him.

"Who is this?" he asked himself. "My niece, who flies away so fast! Niece, let me say a word to you. Where is your husband? If I am dreaming, I would give all my wealth if I could wake up! If I am awake, I wish that some planet would strike me down with its malevolent astrological influence so that I could slumber in eternal sleep! Speak, gentle and kind niece, and tell me what stern and cruel hands have lopped off and hewed and made your body bare of her two branches, those sweet ornaments, in whose circling hugs Kings have sought to sleep? These Kings could never find a happiness that would equal half your love. Why do you not speak to me?"

Lavinia opened her mouth, and blood poured out.

"Alas, a crimson river of warm blood, resembling a bubbling fountain stirred by wind, rises and falls between your rose-red lips, coming and going with your honey-sweet breath. But, surely, some Tereus has raped you, and, lest you should reveal his guilt, he has cut out your tongue.

"Ah, now you turn away your face because of shame! And, notwithstanding all this loss of blood, as from a fountain with three issuing spouts, still your cheeks look as red as the Sun's face when it blushes as it encounters a cloud at dawn or Sunset.

"Shall I speak for you? Shall I say that it is so — that the man who raped you has mutilated you? Oh, I wish that I knew your heart, and I knew the beast, so that I might rant at him and ease my mind!

"Sorrow concealed, like an oven with its door shut, burns the heart to cinders.

"Fair Philomela lost only her tongue after Tereus raped her, but she painstakingly sewed a piece of embroidery that revealed what she had in her mind.

"But, lovely niece, that means of communication is cut from you. You have met a craftier Tereus, niece, and he has cut those pretty fingers off that could have sewed better than Philomela. If the monster had seen your lily-white hands tremble, like aspen-leaves, upon a lute and make the silken strings delight to kiss them, he would not then have touched them for his life!

"Or, if he had heard the Heavenly harmony that your sweet tongue has made, he would have dropped his knife, and fell asleep as Cerberus did at the Thracian poet's feet."

The Thracian poet was Orpheus, who traveled to the Land of the Dead in an attempt to rescue his wife. To get past Cerberus, the three-headed guard dog of Hell, he played his lute and sang. Cerberus, put under a spell by the music, fell asleep.

Marcus Andronicus continued, "Come, let us go, and make your father blind, for such a sight will blind a father's eye. One hour's storm will drown the fragrant meadows. What will whole months of tears do to your father's eyes? Do not draw away from me, for we will mourn with you. Oh, how I wish our mourning could ease your misery!"

He and Lavinia departed.

CHAPTER 3

— 3.1 —

On a street in Rome, Martius and Quintus, guarded and with their hands tied, were being taken to the place of execution. Walking with them were Judges, Senators, and Tribunes. Titus Andronicus was begging for the lives of his sons.

Titus Andronicus begged, "Hear me, grave fathers! Noble Tribunes, stop! Out of pity for my old age, whose youth was spent in dangerous wars while you securely slept, and out of pity for all the blood of my sons that was shed in Rome's great war, and out of pity for all the frosty nights that I have watched on guard, and out of pity for these bitter tears, which you see now filling the aged wrinkles in my cheeks, have pity on my condemned sons, whose souls are not corrupted although people think they are. For twenty-two of my sons, I have never wept because they died honorably."

Titus Andronicus now regarded his son Mutius as having died honorably. Mutius had resisted the will of Saturninus, and Saturninus had now sentenced two of Titus' other sons to death. Also, Mutius had died helping his sister, Lavinia.

Titus fell to the ground. Everyone walked past him, continuing to the place of execution.

He said, "For these two sons, Tribunes, in the dust I write my heart's deep grief and my soul's sad tears. Let my tears quench the earth's dry appetite. My two sons' sweet blood will make the earth shame and blush. Oh, earth, I will befriend you with more rain that shall fall from these two ancient urns than youthful April shall provide with all its showers. In summer's drought I'll drop tears upon you continually. In winter I'll melt the snow with warm tears and keep eternal springtime on your face, provided that you refuse to drink my dear sons' blood."

Lucius, carrying a drawn sword, walked over to his father.

Titus, his head still down, said, "Oh, reverend Tribunes! Oh, gentle, aged men! Unbind my sons, reverse the judgment of death, and let me, who has never wept before, say that my tears are now prevailing orators. Tell me that my tears have been successful at persuading you to pardon the lives of my two sons."

36

Lucius said, "Oh, noble father, you lament in vain. The Tribunes cannot hear you; no man is nearby. You are telling your sorrows to a stone."

"Ah, Lucius, let me plead for your brothers," Titus Andronicus said. "Grave Tribunes, once more I beg of you —"

"My gracious lord, no Tribune hears you speak."

"Why, it does not matter, man," Titus Andronicus said. "If they did hear me, they would ignore me, or if they did pay attention to me, they would not pity me, and yet I must plead; therefore, I tell my sorrows to the stones, which, although they cannot relieve my distress, yet in some ways they are better than the Tribunes because they will not interrupt my tale. When I weep, they humbly at my feet receive my tears and seem to weep with me, and if they were only dressed in solemn clothing, Rome could support no better Tribunes than these. A stone is as soft as wax — Tribunes are harder than stones. A stone is silent, and does not offend, but Tribunes with their tongues condemn men to death."

Titus stood up and asked, "But why are you standing with your weapon drawn?"

"I tried to rescue my two brothers from their deaths," Lucius said. "I failed, and because of my attempt to rescue my brothers the judges have pronounced my everlasting doom of banishment."

"Oh, happy and fortunate man!" Titus Andronicus said. "They have befriended you. Why, foolish Lucius, don't you perceive that Rome is only a wilderness of tigers? Tigers must prey, and Rome affords no prey except for me and mine. How happy and fortunate you are, then, because you are banished from these devourers!"

Titus saw his brother, Marcus, coming toward them. Behind Marcus was a figure that Titus could not see clearly.

Titus asked, "But who is coming here with my brother, Marcus?"

Marcus said, "Titus, prepare your aged eyes to weep, or if you do not do so, prepare your noble heart to break. I bring consuming, devouring sorrow to your old age."

"Will it consume me?" Titus asked. "Let me see it, then."

He was ready for his life to be consumed so that he could die.

"This was your daughter," Marcus said as Lavinia stepped closer.

"Why, Marcus, so she still is."

Seeing Lavinia's bloody stumps, Lucius knelt and said, "This sight kills me!"

Titus said, "Faint-hearted boy, arise, and look upon her."

Lucius got up.

Titus Andronicus said to his daughter, "Speak, Lavinia, what accursed hand has made you handless in your father's sight? What fool has added water to the sea, or brought a faggot to bright-burning Troy? My grief was at the height before you came here to me, and now my grief is like the Nile River, which disdains all bounds — it overflows and floods.

"Give me a sword, and I'll chop off my hands, too, because they have fought for Rome, and all in vain. My hands have also nursed my woe by feeding me and keeping me alive. They have been held up in unavailing prayer, and they have served me ineffectively. Now all the service I require of them is that the one will help to cut off the other.

"It is well, Lavinia, that you have no hands, because hands that do Rome service are useless."

Lucius asked Lavinia, "Speak, gentle sister, who has mutilated you?"

Marcus answered for her: "Oh, that delightful instrument of her thoughts that blabbed them with such pleasing eloquence has been torn from forth that pretty hollow cage, her mouth, where, like a sweet melodious bird, it sang sweet and varied notes, enchanting every ear!"

"Can you say for her who has done this deed?" Lucius asked.

Marcus replied, "I found her like this, straying in the enclosed hunting ground, seeking to hide herself, as does the deer that has received some terminal wound."

Titus said, "Lavinia is my dear, and the man who wounded her has hurt me more than he would have if he had killed me. For now I stand like a man upon a rock surrounded by a wilderness of sea, who sees the incoming tide grow wave by wave, expecting always that some malicious surge of the sea will swallow him in its brinish bowels."

Titus pointed and said, "My wretched sons have traveled down this way to their deaths."

He then said, "Here stands my other son, a banished man, and here is my brother, weeping at my woes. But that which gives my soul the greatest hurt is dear Lavinia, who is dearer than my soul."

He said to her, "Had I but seen your picture in this plight, it would have made me insane. What shall I do now that I behold your living body like this? You have no hands to wipe away your tears, nor a tongue to tell me who has mutilated you. Your husband is dead, and being found guilty of his death, your brothers were condemned to die, and they are dead by this time."

Lavinia expressed her sorrow by crying.

"Look, Marcus!" Titus said. "Ah, son Lucius, look at her! When I mentioned her brothers, then fresh tears fell on her cheeks, like honey-dew falls upon a plucked lily that is almost withered."

Marcus said, "Perhaps she weeps because her brothers killed her husband, or perhaps she weeps because she knows that they are innocent."

Titus said to Lavinia, "If they killed your husband, then be joyful because the law has taken revenge on them."

Then he said, "No, no, they would not do so foul a deed. Witness the sorrow that their sister shows.

"Gentle Lavinia, let me kiss your lips. Or make some sign to me to tell me how I may ease your pain. Shall your good uncle, and your brother Lucius, and you, and I sit round about some fountain, all of us looking downwards at the reflection to see how our cheeks are stained like still-wet meadows that have muddy slime left on them by a flood? And in the fountain shall we gaze so long that the fresh taste is taken from that clear, fresh water and made a brine-pit with our bitter tears?

"Or shall we cut off our hands, like yours?

"Or shall we bite off our tongues, and pass the remainder of our hateful days in mime?

"What shall we do?

"Let us, who have our tongues, plot some device of further misery that will make us wondered at in the times to come."

Lucius said, "Dear father, stop crying. Look at how my wretched sister sobs and weeps at your grief."

Marcus said, "Patience, dear niece. Good Titus, dry your eyes."

He offered Titus his handkerchief.

"Ah, Marcus, Marcus!" Titus said. "Brother, I know well that your handkerchief cannot drink a tear of mine because you, poor man, have drowned it with your own tears."

Pulling out his handkerchief, Lucius said, "My Lavinia, I will wipe your cheeks."

"Look, Marcus, look!" Titus said. "I understand her gestures. If she had a tongue with which to speak, now she would say to her brother what I said to you. His handkerchief, which is soaked with his own true tears, can do no good on her sorrowful cheeks. Oh, what a harmony of woe is this! Our handkerchiefs are as far from being of use to us as Limbo is from the bliss of Heaven!"

Aaron, who was wearing a scimitar by his side, walked over to them.

He said, "Titus Andronicus, my lord the Emperor sends you this message — that, if you love your sons, let Marcus, Lucius, or yourself, old Titus, or any one of you, chop off your hand and send it to the King. In return for the hand, he will send to you here both of your sons alive. The hand shall be the ransom for their crime."

Happy, Titus Andronicus said, "Oh, gracious Emperor! Oh, kind and gentle Aaron! Did a raven ever sing so much like a morning lark that gives sweet tidings of the Sun's rise? With all my heart, I'll send the Emperor my hand. Good Aaron, will you help to chop it off?"

"Stop, father!" Lucius said. "That noble hand of yours, which has thrown down and conquered so many enemies, shall not be sent to the Emperor. My own hand will serve the turn. My youth can better spare my blood than you can spare your blood, and therefore my hand shall save my brothers' lives."

Marcus Andronicus said to Titus and Lucius, "Which of your hands has not defended Rome, and reared aloft the bloody battle-axe to write destruction on the enemy's castle? Oh, both of you deserve so much. My own hand has been entirely idle; let it serve to ransom my two nephews from their deaths. Now I know that I have kept my hand until now so that it can have a worthy end."

Aaron said, "Come, agree quickly whose hand I shall take to the Emperor out of fear that Martius and Quintus will die before their pardon arrives."

"My hand shall go," Marcus said.

"By Heaven, it shall not go!" Lucius said.

"Sirs, argue no more," Titus said. Referring to his hands, he said, "Such withered herbs as these are suitable for being plucked up, and therefore Aaron shall carry my hand to the Emperor."

"Sweet father, if I am to be thought your son," Lucius said, "let me redeem both my brothers from death."

Marcus said to Titus, "And, for our father's sake and mother's care, now let me show you a brother's love."

Titus said, "You two come to an agreement. I will spare my hand."

He was being deliberately ambiguous. Marcus and Lucius thought that the word "spare" meant "leave unharmed," but Titus was using the word "spare" to mean "do without."

"Then I'll go and fetch an axe," Lucius said.

"But I will use the axe to cut off my hand," Marcus said.

Marcus and Lucius departed to get an axe.

"Come here, Aaron," Titus said. "I'll deceive them both. Lend me your hand, and I will give you mine. Help me cut off my hand."

Aaron thought, *If what Titus is doing is called deceit, then I will be an honest man. Never will I deceive men the way that Titus is deceiving these two men. But, you, Titus, I will deceive in a different way, as you will realize before half an hour passes.*

Aaron used his scimitar to cut off Titus' hand at the elbow.

Marcus and Lucius came back.

Titus Andronicus said to them, "Now stop your strife. What had to be done has been done."

He then said, "Good Aaron, give his Majesty my hand. Tell him it was a hand that guarded him from a thousand dangers; bid him bury it. My hand has deserved more and better, but let it at least be buried. As for my sons, say I value them as if they were jewels purchased at an easy and low price, and yet they are dear, too — both loved and expensive — because I bought what was already rightfully mine."

Aaron replied, "I go, Titus Andronicus, and in return for your hand look to have your sons with you soon."

He thought, *Your son's heads, I mean. Oh, how this villainy nourishes and delights me when I merely think of it! Let fools do good, and let fair men call for grace. Aaron prefers to have his soul black like his face.*

He left, carrying Titus' severed left hand.

Titus Andronicus knelt and said, "Here I lift this one hand up to Heaven, and I bow this feeble ruin — my body — to the Earth. If any power pities wretched tears, to that power I call!"

Lavinia knelt.

He said to Lavinia, "What, will you kneel with me? Do, then, dear heart, for Heaven shall hear our prayers or we will breathe foggy sighs and dim the sky, and stain the Sun with fog, as sometimes clouds do when they hug the Sun in their raining bosoms."

Marcus Andronicus said to Titus, "Oh, brother, speak about actions that are possibilities, and do not break into these deep, extreme, and outrageous exaggerations."

"Is not my sorrow deep, because it has no bottom?" Titus replied, "Then my passionate outbursts should be bottomless with them."

"But still let the power of reason govern your laments."

"If there were reasons for these miseries, then I could bind my woes into limits," Titus said. "When Heaven weeps, doesn't the earth overflow? If the winds rage, doesn't the sea grow mad and threaten the sky with his big, swollen waves? And will you have a reason for this turmoil?

"I am the sea; listen, how Lavinia's sighs blow like wind! She is the weeping sky; I am also the earth. My sea must then be moved with her sighs. My earth must then with her continual tears become a flood, overflowed and drowned. This is why my bowels cannot hide her woes, but like a drunkard I must vomit them. So give me leave to speak, for losers will have leave to ease the resentment in their stomachs with their bitter tongues."

A messenger arrived. He was carrying Titus' severed hand and the heads of his sons Martius and Quintus.

The messenger said, "Worthy Titus Andronicus, you are badly repaid for your good hand that you sent to the Emperor. Here are the heads of your two noble sons, and here's your hand, sent back to you in scorn. Your griefs are their entertainment; they mock your resolution. When I think about your woes, I feel more sorrow than I do when I remember my father's death."

The messenger exited.

Marcus Andronicus said, "Now let the hot volcano Aetna cool in Sicily, and let my heart be an ever-burning Hell! These miseries are more than may be endured. To weep with them who weep does ease grief somewhat, but sorrow jeered and mocked at is double death."

Lucius said, "I am amazed that this sight should make so deep a wound, and yet detested life does not shrink away and leave this body dead! I am amazed that death should ever let life bear the name of life, where life does nothing more than breathe!"

Lavinia kissed Titus.

Marcus Andronicus said, "I am sorry, poor heart, but that kiss is as comfortless as frozen water is to a frozen snake."

Titus Andronicus said, "When will this fearful slumber filled with nightmares come to an end?"

Marcus said, "Now, farewell, delusion. Die, Andronicus: You are not sleeping. Look at your two sons' heads, your warlike hand, your mangled daughter here, and your other son, who has been banished and who has been struck pale and bloodless with this grievous sight. And look at me, your brother, who is now like a stony image, cold and numb. Ah, I will now no more curb your griefs. Tear off your silver hair, and gnaw your other hand with your teeth. Let this dismal sight result in the closing up of our most wretched eyes."

Titus was silent.

Marcus said to him, "Now is a time to rant and storm. Why are you silent?"

Titus Andronicus laughed long, loud, and hard.

"Why are you laughing?" Marcus asked. "It is not suitable for this hour."

"Why am I laughing?" Titus replied. "Because I don't have another tear to shed. Besides, this sorrow is an enemy, and would take over my watery eyes and make them blind with tears shed in tribute to my sorrow, and how then shall I find the way to the goddess Revenge's cave? For these two heads of my sons seem to speak to me, and threaten that I shall never come to bliss until all these evils be returned again and thrust down the throats of those who have committed them.

"Come, let me see what task I have to do. You sorrowful people, circle round about me, so that I may turn to each of you, and swear upon my soul to right your wrongs."

He swore the oaths and then said, "The vow is made. Come, brother, take a head, and in this hand I will bear the other head. Lavinia, you shall also be employed. Carry my hand, sweet girl, between your teeth. As for you, Lucius, my boy, get yourself away from my sight: You are an exile, and you must not stay here. Hurry to the Goths, and raise an army there, and, if you love me, as I think you do, let's kiss and part, for we have much to do."

Titus and Lucius kissed each other, and then Titus, Marcus, and Lavinia exited.

Alone, Lucius said, "Farewell, Titus Andronicus, my noble father, the most woeful man who ever lived in Rome. Farewell, proud Rome. Until Lucius comes here again, he leaves his pledges dearer than his life — his loved ones. Farewell, Lavinia, my noble sister. I wish you were as you heretofore have been! But now neither Lucius nor Lavinia lives except in oblivion and hateful griefs. If I, Lucius, shall live, I will requite your wrongs and make proud Saturninus and his Empress beg at the gates, like Tarquin and his Queen."

After King Tarquin's son, who was also named Tarquin, raped Lucrece, who committed suicide, King Tarquin was overthrown. Lucius Junius Brutus led the revolt against King Tarquin.

Lucius continued, "Now I will go to the Goths and raise an army with which I will be revenged on Rome and Saturninus."

— 3.2 —

A light meal was set out on a table in Titus Andronicus' house. Around the table sat Titus Andronicus, Marcus Andronicus, Lavinia, and Lucius' son: young Lucius.

Titus said, "So, so; now sit, and be careful to eat no more than will preserve just so much strength in us that will allow us to revenge these bitter woes of ours."

Titus fed Lavinia during the meal.

He said to his brother, who had folded his arms in front of himself, which was a sign of sorrow, "Marcus, unknit that knot that is a wreath of sorrow. Your niece and I, poor creatures, lack our hands, and cannot passionately express our tenfold grief with folded arms. This poor right hand of mine is left to tyrannize upon my breast; when my heart, all mad with misery, beats in this hollow prison of my flesh, then I use my hand to thump it down."

Titus said to Lavinia, "You map and pattern of woe, who thus talks in signs! When your poor heart beats with extremely violent beating, you cannot strike it like this to make it still.

"Wound it with sighing, girl, kill it with groans, or get some little knife between your teeth, and just against your heart make a hole so that all the tears that your poor eyes let fall may run into and soak that sink, and drown the lamenting sweet fool with sea-salt tears."

"No, brother, no!" Marcus said to Titus, "Don't advise her to lay such violent hands upon her young and tender life."

"What!" Titus replied. "Has sorrow made you deranged already? Why, Marcus, no man but I should be insane. What violent hands can she lay on her life? Ah, why do you mention the word 'hands'? Would you ask Aeneas to twice tell the tale of how Troy was burnt and he was made miserable? Oh, don't discuss the theme of hands, lest we remember now that we have none. Oh, how stupid it is to regulate talk, as if we should forget we had no hands if Marcus did not say the word 'hands'!

"Come, let's fall to the meal; and, gentle girl, Lavinia, eat this."

Titus, noticing that the servants had forgotten to bring in something to drink, said, "Here is no drink!"

Lavinia indicated with gestures that she did not need anything to drink and Titus said, "Pay attention, Marcus, to what she is saying. I can interpret all her mutilated and tortured signs. She says she drinks no other drink but tears, brewed with her sorrow, fermented upon her cheeks."

He said to Lavinia, "Speechless complainer, I will learn your thought. In interpreting your mime, I will be as perfect as begging hermits are in their holy prayers. They are word-perfect in saying their prayers, and I will be word-perfect in interpreting your gestures. You shall not sigh, nor hold your stumps up to Heaven, nor close your eyes, nor nod, nor kneel, nor make a sign, but I will wrest an alphabet from your gestures and by constant practice learn to know your meaning."

Young Lucius said to Titus, "Good Grandfather, stop making these bitter deep laments; instead, make my aunt merry with some pleasing tale."

Marcus said, "Alas, the young and tender boy, moved by strong emotion, weeps to see his grandfather's misery."

"Be at peace, tender sapling," Titus said to young Lucius. "You are full of tears, and tears will quickly melt your life away."

Marcus struck at his dish with a knife.

Titus asked, "What did you strike at, Marcus, with your knife?"

"I struck at something that I have killed, my lord: a fly."

"Get out, murderer!" Titus said. "You kill my heart. My eyes are gorged with sights of tyranny. It is not fitting for Titus' brother to commit a deed of death on the innocent. Get out! I see you are not fit for my company."

Marcus said, "My lord, I have killed only a fly."

Titus said, "'Only'? But what if that fly had a father and a mother? How would the father hang his slender gilded wings and buzz sad laments in the air! Poor harmless fly, that, with his pretty buzzing melody, came here to make us merry! And you have killed him."

"Pardon me, sir," Marcus said. "It was a black, ugly, ill-favored fly that looked like the Empress' Moor; therefore, I killed him."

"Oh," Titus said. "Then pardon me for reprimanding you, because you have done a charitable deed. Give me your knife; I will triumph over him, pretending to myself that it is the Moor, who has come here intending to poison me."

Titus took the knife and stabbed at the dead fly, saying, "There's for yourself, and that's for Tamora. Ah, sirrah! I think that we are not yet brought so low that between us we cannot kill a fly that comes to us in the likeness of a coal-black Moor."

Marcus said to himself, "Poor man! Grief has so stricken him that he thinks that false shadows are true substances."

"Come, take away the meal," Titus said. "Lavinia, come with me. I'll go to your private chamber and read to you sad stories that happened in the days of old. Come, boy, and go with me. Your sight is young, and you shall read when my sight begins to be dazzled."

CHAPTER 4

— 4.1 —

In Titus' garden in Rome, Lavinia ran after young Lucius, who was carrying books under his arm. Titus and Marcus entered the garden and saw them.

Young Lucius dropped his books and ran to Titus and Marcus, yelling, "Help, Grandfather, help! My aunt Lavinia follows me everywhere, I don't know why. Good uncle Marcus, see how swiftly she comes. Alas, sweet aunt, I don't know what you want."

"Stand by me, Lucius," Marcus said. "Do not fear your aunt."

"She loves you, boy, too well to do you harm," Titus said.

"Yes, when my father was in Rome, she loved me," young Lucius said.

"What does my niece Lavinia mean by these gestures she is making?" Marcus asked.

"Don't be afraid of her, young Lucius," Titus said. "She means something. See, young Lucius, see how much she gestures to you. She would have you go somewhere with her. Ah, boy, Cornelia never with more care read to her sons than Lavinia has read to you sweet poetry and Cicero's book *Orator*."

Cornelia Africana's sons, whom she educated well, were known as the Gracchi. They were social reformers of Rome when Rome was a republic.

"Can't you guess why Lavinia keeps at you like this?" Marcus asked.

"My lord, I don't know, nor can I guess, unless some fit or frenzy is possessing her. I have heard my grandfather say very often that an extremity of griefs would make men mad, and I have read that Queen Hecuba of Troy became insane through sorrow after Troy fell and so many of her children died.

"My lord, although I know my noble aunt loves me as dearly as my mother ever did, and would not, except in delirium, frighten my youth, I was frightened, which made me throw down my books, and run away — without a good reason to, perhaps.

"But pardon me, sweet aunt. And, madam, if my uncle Marcus goes with me, I will most willingly go with your ladyship."

"Young Lucius, I will go with you," Marcus said.

Lavinia and the others went to the books that young Lucius had dropped, and Lavinia began to look through them, moving them with her stumps.

Titus Andronicus said, "How are you, Lavinia! What are you doing? Marcus, what does this mean? She wants to see a particular book.

"Which is it, girl, of these? Open them, boy. But you, Lavinia, are deeper read, and better skilled at reading, and can read harder books than young Lucius. Come, Lavinia, and take your choice of all the books in my library, and so forget for a while your sorrow, until the Heavens reveal the damned contriver of this evil deed."

Lavinia raised her stumps.

Titus asked, "Why is she lifting up her arms like this now?"

Marcus answered, "I think she means that there was more than one confederate in the crime. Yes, there was more than one, or else she heaves her arms to Heaven as a way of asking for revenge."

Titus asked, "Young Lucius, what book is that she is tossing about?"

"Grandfather, it is Ovid's *Metamorphoses*. My mother gave it to me."

Marcus said, "Perhaps she selected it from among the rest for the love of her who is gone."

"Look!" Titus said. "See how busily she turns the pages!"

He helped her turn the pages and asked, "What is she looking for?"

Lavinia stopped at a passage in the *Metamorphoses*.

Titus said, "This is Ovid's account of the tragic tale of Philomela. It tells about Tereus' treason and his rape. And rape, I fear, is the root of your distress."

"Look, brother, look," Marcus said. "Note how she closely observes the pages."

Titus asked, "Lavinia, were you attacked, sweet girl, raped, and wronged, as Philomela was, and forced to have sex in the ruthless, desolate, and gloomy woods?"

She nodded, and Titus said, "See, see! Yes, such a place there is, where we hunted — oh, I wish that we had never, never hunted there! That place was just like the place that the poet here describes; nature made that place for murders and rapes."

Marcus Andronicus asked, "Why should nature build so foul a den, unless the gods delight in tragedies?"

Titus said to Lavinia, "Give us signs, sweet girl, for here are none but friends. With signs let us know which Roman lord it was who dared to do the evil deed. Did Saturninus slink — it is possible that he did — as Tarquin did formerly when he slunk out of the military camp to commit rape in Lucrece's bed?"

Marcus said, "Sit down, sweet niece. Brother, sit down by me. Apollo, Pallas, Jove, or Mercury, inspire me so that I may find who did this treason!

"My lord, look here. Look here, Lavinia: This sandy plot of land is level. Lavinia, guide, if you can, my staff. Watch me and then imitate me. I will use my staff to write my name without the help of any hand at all."

He held one end of the staff in his mouth and used his feet to guide the other end of the staff and write his name in the sand.

He said, "Cursed be that heart that forced us to this makeshift!

"Write, you good niece, and here display, at last, what God wants to be revealed so that we may take revenge. May Heaven guide your pen to print your sorrows plainly so that we may know the traitors and the truth!"

Lavinia took one end of the staff in her mouth, and she used her stumps to write with the staff.

Titus said, "Do you read, my lord, what she has written? '*Stuprum*. Chiron. Demetrius.'"

The word *Stuprum* is Latin for "Rape." Lavinia had succeeded in telling Titus and Marcus that Chiron and Demetrius had raped her.

Marcus said, "What! The lustful sons of Tamora are guilty of this heinous, bloody deed?"

Titus said, "*Magni Dominator poli, tam lentus audis scelera, tam lentus vides?*"

This is Latin for "Ruler of the great heavens, are you so slow to hear crimes, so slow to see them?" Titus was quoting a passage from the Roman playwright Seneca's tragedy *Hippolytus*.

Marcus said to Titus, "Calm yourself, gentle lord, although I know enough is written upon this earth in front of us to stir a rebellion in the mildest thoughts and arm the minds of infants to make outcries of protest.

"My lord, kneel down with me; Lavinia, kneel; and kneel, sweet boy, the Roman Hector's hope."

They knelt.

Hector was the foremost Trojan warrior; his hope was his son. Marcus was calling the elder Lucius the Roman Hector.

Near the end of the Trojan War, Achilles killed Hector. After Troy fell, Hector's young son was killed by being thrown from the high walls of Troy.

Marcus said, "Swear with me, as, along with the woe-stricken spouse and father of that chaste dishonored dame, Lucrece, Lucius Junius Brutus swore for her rape, that we will pursue a good plan to get deadly revenge upon these traitorous Goths, and see their blood, or else we will die with this disgrace."

They swore and rose.

"Revenge is certain, if you know how to get it," Titus said. "But if you hunt these bear-cubs, then beware. The dam will wake up; and, if she once catches your scent ... she's still deeply in league with the lion, and lulls him while she plays sexually on her back, and when he sleeps she does whatever — and whoever — she wishes."

The dam, of course, is Tamora, and the bear-cubs are her rapist sons.

Titus continued, "You are an inexperienced huntsman, Marcus, so leave the plot to me. Come, I will go and get a leaf of brass, and with a pen of steel I will write these words on it, and store it. That will make our oath of revenge permanent.

"The angry northern wind will blow these sands, like the Sibyl's leaves, abroad, and where's your lesson, then?"

The Sibyl was a prophetess who wrote her prophecies on leaves that the wind scattered.

Titus asked, "Boy, what do you have to say?"

Young Lucius replied, "I say, my lord, that if I were a man, not even their mother's bedchamber would be a safe harbor for these bad men — these slaves who are under the yoke of Rome."

Marcus said, "Yes, that's my boy! Your father has very often done the like for his ungrateful country."

"And, uncle, so will I, if I live," young Lucius said.

"Come, go with me into my armory," Titus said. "Young Lucius, I'll outfit you; and my boy, you shall carry from me to the Empress' sons presents that I intend to send to both of them. Come, come; you'll deliver the message, won't you?"

"Yes, with my dagger in their bosoms, Grandfather."

"No, boy, no," Titus said. "I'll teach you another course of action. Lavinia, come. Marcus, look after my house. Young Lucius and I will go and swagger at the court. Yes, by the virgin Mary, we will, sir; and we'll not be ignored."

Titus, Lavinia, and young Lucius exited.

Marcus Andronicus, who felt that Titus was exhibiting signs of insanity and therefore would not be able to get revenge, said to himself, "Heavens, can you hear a good man groan, and not relent or feel compassion for him? I, Marcus, will attend Titus in his bout of insanity. He has more scars of sorrow in his heart than enemy soldiers' marks upon his battered shield, but yet he is so just that he will not get revenge. Get revenge, Heavens, for old Titus Andronicus!"

— 4.2 —

In a room in the palace, Aaron, Demetrius, and Chiron were talking when young Lucius, with an attendant carrying a bundle, entered the room. The bundle consisted of weapons with a scroll of writing wrapped around them.

Chiron, who like the others had heard rumors of Titus Andronicus' insanity, said, "Demetrius, here's the son of Lucius. He has some message to deliver to us."

Aaron said, "Yes, some mad message from his mad grandfather."

Young Lucius, who had heard the comment, said, "My lords, with all the humbleness I may, I greet your honors from Titus Andronicus."

He thought, *And I pray that the Roman gods destroy both of you!*

"Thank you, lovely young Lucius," Demetrius said. "What's the news?"

Young Lucius thought, *The news is that we now know that you two villains have committed rape and mutilation.*

He said out loud, "May it please you, my grandfather, who is sound of mind, has sent by me the best weapons from his armory to please you honorable youths, who are the hope of Rome — so he told me to say, and so I say it. He wanted me to present your lordships with these gifts of weapons so that, whenever you have need to be, you will be well armed and well equipped, and so I now leave you both."

The attendant handed over the gift of weapons, and young Lucius thought, *And so I now leave you both, Demetrius and Chiron, you bloody villains.*

Young Lucius and the attendant exited.

Demetrius said, "What's this? A scroll, with words written round about it? Let's see."

He read out loud, "*Integer vitae, scelerisque purus, non eget Mauri jaculis, nec arcu.*"

This is Latin for "He who is of upright life and free from crime does not need the javelins or the bow of the Moor."

Chiron said, "Oh, it is a verse in Horace; I know it well. I read it in my grammar book long ago."

The passage is a quotation from Horace's *Odes*, I, xxii, 1-2.

"Yes, correct," Aaron said. "It is a verse in Horace; right, you have it."

He thought, *What a thing it is to be an ass! Here's no sound jest — this is not at all a joke! Titus Andronicus, that old man, has discovered their guilt, and he sends them weapons wrapped about with a scroll containing a message that wounds to the quick although Demetrius and Chiron are too stupid to feel it. If our intelligent Empress were up and about instead of giving birth, she would applaud Andronicus' ingenuity, but I will let her rest in her unrest for a while longer.*

Aaron said out loud, "And now, young lords, wasn't it a happy star that led us to Rome, although we were strangers, and more than that, we were captives, and we have advanced to this height? It did me good before the palace gate to defy Marcus the Tribune in his brother Titus' hearing."

Demetrius said, "But it does me more good to see so great a lord as Titus basely curry favor with us by sending us gifts."

He thought that Titus had given them the weapons as a way of gaining entry into the royal court.

Aaron said, "Doesn't he have a good reason to give you gifts, Lord Demetrius? Didn't you treat his daughter in a very friendly way?"

Demetrius replied, "I wish we had a thousand Roman dames cornered in a desolate place so that they would be forced to take turns satisfying our lust."

Chiron said, "That is a charitable wish and full of love."

Aaron said, "All that is lacking is for your mother to say 'amen' and give you her blessing."

"And she would do that even if we wished for twenty thousand more Roman dames," Chiron said.

"Come, let us go and pray to all the gods for our beloved mother in her pains of childbirth," Demetrius said.

Aaron thought, *Pray to the devils; the gods have abandoned us. Titus Andronicus knows who raped and mutilated Lavinia.*

Trumpets sounded.

"Why do the Emperor's trumpets sound like this?" Demetrius asked.

"Probably for joy," Chiron said. "Probably the Emperor has a son."

Demetrius said, "Quiet! Who is coming toward us?"

A nurse entered the room. In her arms, she carried a newly born black infant: a boy.

"Good morning, lords," the nurse said. "Tell me, have you seen Aaron the Moor?"

Aaron answered, "Well, more or less, or never a whit at all."

He added, "Here Aaron is: I am he. What do you want with Aaron?"

"Oh, gentle Aaron, we are all undone and ruined!" the nurse said. "Now help us, or may woe overwhelm you forevermore!"

"Why, what a caterwauling you keep up!" Aaron said to her. "What do you have so clumsily wrapped in your arms?"

"I have that which I would hide from the eyes of Heaven. I have our Empress' shame, and stately Rome's disgrace! She is delivered, lords; she is delivered."

"Delivered?" Aaron said. "To whom?"

"I mean that she has given birth," the nurse said.

"Well, God give her good rest! What has God sent her?" Aaron said.

"A devil."

This society regarded the devil as being the color black.

"Why, then she is the devil's dam; this is a joyful issue."

"A joyless, dismal, black, and sorrowful issue," the nurse said. "Here is the babe, as loathsome as a toad among the light-complexioned parents of our land. The Empress sends it to you. This babe is your stamp, your seal, your issue, and she bids you to christen it with your dagger's point."

The Empress Tamora wanted Aaron to kill his own child. If the Emperor Saturninus were to see the child, he would know immediately that he was not the father and that Tamora had cheated on him.

"Damn, you whore!" Aaron said. "Is black so base a color?"

He looked at his son and said, "Sweet blowse, you are a beauteous blossom, to be sure."

A "blowse" was a red-faced girl. Of course, Aaron was speaking ironically.

Demetrius and Chiron knew immediately that Aaron had fathered the infant.

"Villain, what have you done?" Demetrius said.

"I have done that which you can not undo," Aaron replied.

"You have undone our mother," Chiron said. "You have ruined her reputation. Now the Emperor will know that she has been unfaithful to him."

"Villain, I have done your mother," Aaron said. "I have slept with her."

"And therein, Hellish dog, you have undone her," Demetrius said. "Woe to her luck, and may her loathed choice be damned! The offspring of so foul a fiend is cursed!"

"The infant shall not live," Chiron said.

"The infant shall not die," Aaron said.

"Aaron, it must die," the nurse said. "The mother wants it to be killed."

"What! Must it be killed, nurse?" Aaron said. "Then let no man but I execute my flesh and blood."

He meant that no man would execute his flesh and blood — he certainly would not.

"I'll pierce the tadpole on my rapier's point," Demetrius said. "Nurse, give it to me; my sword shall soon dispatch and kill it."

"Sooner than that, this sword shall plow your bowels up," Aaron said as he took the infant from the nurse and drew his sword.

"Stop, murderous villains!" Aaron shouted. "Will you kill your brother? Now, by the burning candles of the sky that shone so brightly when this boy was conceived, whoever touches this my first-born son and heir dies upon my scimitar's sharp point. I tell you, youngsters, that the giant Enceladus, with all his threatening band of the giant Typhon's giant brood — all of whom threatened the Olympic gods — shall not seize this prey out of his father's hands. And neither great Hercules nor the war-god Mars shall seize this prey out of his father's hands.

"What! What! You red-faced, shallow-hearted boys! You white-limed walls! You alehouse painted signs! You are copies of men — not real men! Coal-black is better than another hue because it scorns to bear another hue — black cloth cannot be dyed another color. All the water in the ocean can never turn the swan's black legs white, although the sea washes them hourly in the tide.

"Tell the Empress from me that I am of an age to keep what is my own, excuse it how she can."

"Will you betray your noble mistress in this way?" Demetrius asked.

"My mistress is my mistress," Aaron replied. "This infant is myself, the vigor and the picture of my youth. I prefer this infant to all of the world. I will keep this infant safe in spite of all the world, or some of you shall smoke for it in Rome."

The word "smoke" was a metaphor for "be punished." The metaphor came from the smoke arising from a burning at the stake.

"By this our mother is forever shamed," Demetrius said.

"Rome will despise her for this foul sexual escapade," Chiron said.

"The Emperor, in his rage, will sentence the Empress to death," Demetrius said.

"I blush when I think about this ignominy," Chiron said.

"Why, there's the privilege your fair beauty bears," Aaron said. "A white face can blush. White is a treacherous hue that will betray with blushing the secret resolutions and counsels of the heart!"

Referring to his infant son, he said, "Here's a young lad framed of another leer. Look at how the black slave smiles upon the father, as if he should say, 'Old lad, I am your own.' He is your brother, lords, clearly nourished with that blood that first gave life to you, and from that same womb where you were imprisoned, he is freed and come to light.

"Certainly, he is your brother by the surer side, although my seal is stamped in his face."

The surer side is the mother's. In the days before DNA testing, people could be sure who a child's mother is, but because of the existence of cheating wives, people could not always be certain who the child's father is.

"Aaron, what shall I say to the Empress?" the nurse asked.

"Advise us, Aaron, what is to be done," Demetrius said. "And we will all subscribe to your advice. Save the child, as long as we may all be safe."

"Then let us sit down, and let us all consult," Aaron said. "My son and I will keep downwind of you. Stay there."

Aaron was mistrustful. He wanted to keep Demetrius and Chiron at a distance from him and his son in order to protect his son's life.

Demetrius and Chiron sat down.

Aaron then said, "Now we can talk as we wish about your safety."

"How many women saw this child of Aaron's?" Demetrius asked.

"Why, that's the way to act, brave lords!" Aaron said. "When we join together in league, I am a lamb, but if you challenge and defy the Moor, then the angered boar, the mountain lioness, the ocean swells not as much as Aaron storms. You asked a good question. But let me ask it again: How many saw the child?"

"Cornelia the midwife and myself," the nurse replied. "And no one else but the Empress who gave birth to it."

"The Empress, the midwife, and yourself," Aaron said. "Two may keep a secret when the third's away. Go to the Empress, and tell her I said this."

He killed the nurse.

Aaron imitated the sounds the nurse made as she died and said, "So cries a pig when it is being prepared to be spitted and roasted."

Demetrius and Chiron jumped up.

Demetrius asked, "What do you mean by this, Aaron? Why did you do this?"

"Oh, Lord, sir, it is a deed of policy," Aaron replied. "It is part of a plan. Should the nurse — a long-tongued babbling gossip — live to betray this guilt of ours? No, lords, no. And now I will tell you my full plan. Not far away from here, a man named Muli lives. He is my countryman, and his wife just last night gave birth. His child looks like her; his child is as fair and white as you are. Go and make an agreement with him, and give the mother gold. Tell them everything, and tell them that their child shall be advanced in life — it will be treated as and believed to be the Emperor's heir. You can substitute their infant for mine and so calm this tempest whirling in the court. Let the Emperor dandle their son on his knee as he thinks that it is his own son."

Aaron added, "Look, lords; you see that I have given the nurse medicine. And you must now provide a funeral for her. The fields are near, and you are gallant fellows. Once she has been buried, don't waste time but make sure that you send the midwife immediately to me. Once the midwife and the nurse are dead, then let the court ladies gossip as they please."

Aaron had said, "Two may keep a secret when the third's away," but he preferred this proverb: "Three may keep a secret if two of them are dead."

"Aaron, I see that you will not trust even the air with secrets," Chiron said.

"For this taking care of Tamora, she and hers are highly bound to you," Demetrius said.

Demetrius and Chiron carried away the corpse of the nurse.

Alone, Aaron said, "Now I will go to the Goths as swiftly as a swallow flies. There I will dispose of this treasure — my infant — that I am holding in my arms, and I will secretly greet the Empress' friends."

He said tenderly to his infant son, "Come on, you thick-lipped slave, I'll carry you away from here because it is you who puts us to our makeshifts. I'll make you feed on berries and on roots, and feed on curds and whey, and suck goats' milk, and take shelter in a cave, and I will bring you up to be a warrior and command a military camp."

— 4.3 —

Titus Andronicus had prepared several arrows by attaching letters to them. With him were Marcus Andronicus, young Lucius, Publius (Marcus' son), and two kinsmen of the Andronici: Sempronius and Caius. They were carrying bows. Other gentlemen were also present. Some people were carrying nets and tools.

"Come, Marcus; come, kinsmen," Titus said. "This is the way. Sir boy, now let me see your archery. Make sure that you draw the bow fully, and the arrow will arrive at its destination immediately."

He then said, "*Terras Astraea reliquit.*"

Terras Astraea reliquit is Latin for "Astraea, the goddess of justice, has left the Earth."

Titus said, "Remember, Marcus, the goddess of justice is gone — she's fled."

He then ordered, "Sirs, take you to your tools. You, kinsmen, shall go and search the ocean, and cast your nets. Perhaps, and happily, you may catch her in the sea. Yet there's as little justice in the sea as on land.

"Publius and Sempronius, you must dig with mattock and with spade, and pierce the inmost center of the earth. Then, when you come to Pluto's region — the Land of the Dead — then please give him this petition. Tell him that the petition asks for justice and for aid and that it comes from old Titus Andronicus, who is shaken with sorrows in ungrateful Rome.

"Ah, Rome! Well, well; I made you miserable that time I threw the people's votes to him — Saturninus — who thus tyrannizes over me."

He said to some other gentlemen, "Go, get you gone; and please be careful, all of you, and leave not a man-of-war ship unsearched. This wicked Emperor may have shipped the goddess of justice away from here; and, kinsmen, if that is true then we may go and whistle for justice — we won't find the goddess."

Believing that Titus' words showed that he was insane, Marcus said to his son, "Publius, isn't this so sad — to see your noble uncle thus mentally disturbed?"

Publius replied, "Therefore, my lord, we must by day and night take care to always be near him and to indulge his mood as kindly as we can until time produces some healing remedy."

Marcus said, "Kinsmen, Titus' sorrows are past remedy. But let us live in hope that Lucius will join with the Goths and with war take revenge for this ingratitude and wreak vengeance on the traitor Saturninus."

Titus said, "Publius, how are you now! How are you now, my masters! Have you met with the goddess of justice?"

"No, my good lord," Publius replied, "but Pluto sends you word that if you want to have the goddess Revenge come from Hell, you shall get what you want. But as for Justice, she is so employed, he thinks, with Jove in Heaven, or somewhere else, that you must necessarily wait a while longer."

"Pluto does me wrong to feed me with delays," Titus said. "I'll dive into the burning lake below in Hell, and pull the goddess of justice out of Acheron by the heels.

"Marcus, we are only shrubs — no cedars are we."

Titus was alluding to this proverb: "High cedars fall when low shrubs remain."

He continued: "We are not big-boned men framed with the size of the one-eyed giants called the Cyclopes, but we are metal, Marcus. We are steel to our backs. Yet we are wrung with more wrongs than our backs can bear. And, since there's no justice on Earth or in Hell, we will solicit Heaven and move the gods to send down Justice so she can avenge our wrongs.

"Come, let's attend to this business. You are a good archer, Marcus."

Titus handed the others the arrows he had prepared, and he said these things:

"The arrow with the letter to Jove, that's for you.

"Here you are, the arrow with the letter to Apollo.

"The arrow with the letter to Mars, that's for myself.

"Here, boy, the arrow with the letter to Pallas Athena.

"Here, the arrow with the letter to Mercury.

"This is the arrow with the letter to Saturn, Caius — the letter is not to Saturninus. You might as well shoot against the wind as ask Saturninus for justice.

"Way to go, boy!

"Marcus, let loose your arrow when I tell you to.

"On my word, I have written to good effect. There's not a god that I have left unsolicited."

Marcus ordered quietly, "Kinsmen, shoot all your arrows into the courtyard of Saturninus' palace. We will afflict the Emperor in his pride."

Titus' own words showed that his plan was to have everyone shoot the arrows to the constellations so that the gods could read the letters attached to the arrows.

Titus ordered, "Now, masters, draw your bows."

They all shot their arrows.

"Oh, well done, young Lucius!" Titus said. "Good boy, you shot your arrow into Virgo's lap; you gave it to Pallas Athena."

Virgo is the constellation of the Virgin in the Zodiac. Astraea, the goddess of justice, was the last god to leave Humankind. She lived on Earth during the Golden Age, but when Humankind became wicked, she fled to the sky and became the constellation Virgo. Like Pallas Athena, she was a virgin goddess.

Marcus said, "My lord, I aimed a mile beyond the Moon; your letter is with Jupiter by this time."

Titus laughed and said, "Publius, Publius, what have you done? See, see, you have shot off one of Taurus' horns."

Taurus is the constellation of the Bull. Aries is the constellation of the Ram.

"This is entertaining, my lord," Marcus said. "When Publius shot the arrow, the Bull, being scratched, gave Aries such a knock that both the Ram's horns fell down into the courtyard. And who should find them but the Empress' villain: Aaron? The Empress laughed, and told the Moor he should give the horns to his master — Saturninus — for a present."

In other words, Aaron had cuckolded Saturninus and given him metaphorical horns.

"Why, there the horns go," Titus said. "May God give his lordship — Saturninus — joy with his present!"

A rustic man, aka yokel, who carried two pigeons in a basket, walked over to them.

Titus said, "News, news from Heaven! Marcus, the postman has come."

He said to the yokel, "Sirrah, what are the tidings? What is the news? Have you any letters for me? Shall I have justice? What does Jupiter say?"

"Oh, the gibbet-maker!" the yokel said, mistaking "Jupiter" for "gibbiter." A gibbet is a gallows.

The yokel continued, "He says that he has taken the gallows down again, for the man must not be hanged until next week."

Titus asked, "But I am asking you what does Jupiter say?"

"Alas, sir, I know not Jubiter; I never drank with him in all my life," the yokel replied.

"Why, villain, aren't you the letter-carrier?" Titus asked.

"I am a carrier, sir, but of pigeons, not of letters," the yokel replied. "I carry nothing but pigeons."

"Why, didn't you come from Heaven?"

"From Heaven! Alas, sir, I never came there. God forbid that I should be so bold as to press my way to Heaven in my young days. When I am older, I hope to go to Heaven. Why, right now I am going with my pigeons to the *tribunal plebs*, to take up a matter of a brawl between my uncle and one of the emperial's men."

The yokel misused words. By *tribunal plebs*, he meant *tribunus plebis*, which is Latin for "Tribune of the Common People." He was carrying the pigeons as a gift, aka bribe, to the Tribune so that he would help his uncle resolve the case. By "emperial's," he meant "Emperor's."

Marcus said to Titus, "Why, sir, this man is as suitable as can be to deliver your petition; let him deliver the pigeons to the Emperor from you."

Titus asked the yokel, "Tell me, can you with grace deliver a petition to right a wrong to the Emperor?"

By "with grace," Titus meant "gracefully," but the yokel understood it to mean "with a prayer before a meal."

The yokel replied, "No, truly, sir, I could never say grace in all my life."

"Sirrah, come here," Titus said to the yokel. "Make no more trouble, but give your pigeons to the Emperor. By me you shall have justice at his hands. Wait, wait; meanwhile, here's money for your expenses."

Titus gave him some money and then said, "Get me a pen and some ink."

He then said to the yokel, "Sirrah, can you with grace deliver a petition?"

With money in his hand, the yokel replied, "Yes, sir."

"Then here is a petition for you to deliver. And when you come to the Emperor, at the first approach you must kneel, then kiss his foot, then deliver up your pigeons, and then look for your reward. I'll be at hand, sir; see you do it with a fine flourish."

"I promise you that I will, sir. Leave it to me."

Titus asked, "Sirrah, have you a knife?"

The yokel indicated that he had a knife, and Titus said, "Come, let me see it."

Titus took the knife and then said, "Here, Marcus, fold the petition around it."

After Marcus was done, Titus handed the petition and the knife to the yokel and said, "You must hold it like a humble suppliant. After you have given it to the Emperor, come and knock at my door, and tell me what he says."

"May God be with you, sir; I will."

Titus said, "Come, Marcus, let us go. Publius, follow me."

— 4.4 —

In a room of the palace were Saturninus, Tamora, Demetrius, Chiron, and some lords and attendants.

Holding in his hand the arrows that Titus Andronicus and his kinsmen had shot, Saturninus said, "Why, lords, what insults are these! Was there ever seen an Emperor in Rome thus put down, troubled, and confronted like this, and, because he has dispensed justice fairly and evenly, treated with such contempt?

"My lords, you know, as do the mighty gods — no matter how much these disturbers of our peace buzz lies in the people's ears — that nothing has occurred except what is in accordance with the law against the headstrong sons of old Titus Andronicus. And so what if his sorrows have so overwhelmed his wits and sanity? Shall we be thus afflicted and suffer because of his vengeance, his fits, his frenzy, and his bitterness?

61

"And now Titus writes to Heaven to redress the wrongs he claims were done to him. See, here's a letter to Jove, and this letter is to Mercury. This letter is to Apollo; this letter is to the god of war. These are sweet scrolls to fly about the streets of Rome!

"What's this but libel against the Senate, and proclaiming everywhere what Titus considers to be our injustice? A goodly sentiment, is it not, my lords? He would say that no justice is in Rome.

"But if I live, his feigned madness shall be no shelter to allow him to commit these outrages without being punished. He and his kinsmen shall know that justice lives in Saturninus' health. If justice sleeps, he will so awake her that she in fury shall cut down the proudest conspirator who lives."

Tamora said, "My gracious lord, my lovely Saturninus, lord of my life, commander of my thoughts, be calm, and bear the faults of Titus' age, the effects of sorrow for his valiant sons, whose loss has pierced him deep and scarred his heart. Instead, comfort his distressed plight rather than prosecute the lowest- or the highest-ranking for these acts of contempt toward you."

She thought, *Why, it shall be best if quick-witted Tamora speaks fair — but false — words about everyone. But, Titus, I have touched you to the quick. Your life-blood is pouring out. If Aaron will now be wise and kill his and my child, then all is safe — the anchor's in the port.*

The yokel entered the room and Tamora said to him, "How are you now, good fellow! Do you want to speak with us?"

"Yes, indeed, if your mistress-ship is emperial."

"I am the Empress, but yonder sits the Emperor."

"It is he," the yokel said.

He said to Saturninus, "May God and Saint Stephen give you a good day. I have brought you a letter and a couple of pigeons here."

Saturninus took the letter and read it, and then he ordered, "Go and take this rustic fellow away, and hang him immediately."

Mishearing "hung" as "hand," the yokel asked, "How much money will I be handed?"

Tamora said, "Come, sirrah, you must be hanged."

"Hanged!" the yokel said. "By our lady, then I have brought up a neck to a fair end. My neck and my legal case both come to an end."

Guards took away the yokel.

Saturninus complained, "Despiteful and intolerable wrongs! Shall I endure this monstrous villainy? I know from whence this plot proceeds. Must I endure this? Titus believes that his traitorous sons, who died lawfully for the murder of our brother, have by my means been butchered wrongfully!

"Go and drag the villain Titus here by his hair. Neither old age nor honor shall confer immunity on him. Because of this proud insult of his, I'll be his butcher. He is a sly frantic wretch who helped to make me great, in hopes that he would rule both Rome and me."

Aemilius, a noble Roman, entered the room.

Saturninus asked, "What news have you brought, Aemilius?"

"Prepare for war, my lord — Rome never had more reason to do so. The Goths have gathered soldiers, and with an army of highly determined men who are resolved to plunder Rome, they are quickly marching here under the leadership of Lucius, son to old Andronicus. Lucius threatens, in the course of this revenge, to do as much as ever Coriolanus did."

Coriolanus had been a heroic warrior and general for Rome, but he ended up leading an enemy army against Rome.

Saturninus asked, "Is warlike Lucius the general of the Goths? These tidings nip me the way that a gardener pinches off the buds of a plant, and I hang my head as flowers do with frost or grass that is beaten down with storms.

"Yes, now our sorrows begin to approach. Lucius is the man the common people love so much. I myself have often overheard them say, when I have walked in their midst while disguised like a private man, that Lucius was wrongfully banished. I have heard them say that they wished that Lucius were their Emperor."

Tamora said, "Why should you fear the invading army? Is not your city strong?"

"Yes, but the citizens favor Lucius, and they will revolt from me and aid him."

Tamora said, "King, let your thoughts be imperious, like your name. The name 'Saturninus' comes from the name of the god Saturn. Is the Sun dimmed when gnats fly in its beams? The eagle allows little birds to sing and does not care what they mean when they sing because the eagle knows that with the shadow of his wings he can, whenever he wishes, stop their melody. Like the eagle, you can stop the frivolous and irresponsible men of Rome. So cheer up your spirit.

"Know, Emperor, that I will enchant old Titus Andronicus with words that are more sweet, and yet more dangerous, than bait is to fish, or honey-stalks to sheep. The fish are wounded with the bait, and the sheep are rotted with excessive consumption of the delicious honey-stalks."

This society believed that sheep became bloated and died from liver rot when they overfed on honey-stalks.

"But Titus will not ask his son not to attack us," Saturninus said.

"If I, Tamora, ask Titus to do that, then he will. For I can sooth and flatter and fill his aged ear with golden promises, with the result that, even if his heart were almost impregnable and his old ears were deaf, his ears and his heart would still obey my tongue. Titus will do whatever I ask him to do — I can be very persuasive."

She said to Aemilius, "Go to Lucius now and be our ambassador to him. Say that the Emperor requests a parley with warlike Lucius, and set up the meeting at the house of his father, old Titus Andronicus."

Saturninus said, "Aemilius, honorably deliver this message. And if he insists on hostages to ensure his safety, ask him to identify which hostages will please him best."

"I shall earnestly do as you wish," Aemilius said, and he exited.

Tamora said, "Now I will go to old Titus Andronicus, and manipulate him with all the art I have so that we can pluck proud Lucius from the warlike Goths.

"And now, sweet Emperor, be blithe and happy again, and bury all your fear and have faith in my plan."

Emperor Saturninus replied, "Go immediately to Titus, and plead with him."

CHAPTER 5

— 5.1 —

Near Rome, Lucius talked to some of the Goths in his army.

He said, "Proven warriors, and my faithful friends, I have received letters from great Rome, which tell how the Romans hate their Emperor and how desirous they are to see us. Therefore, great lords, be, as your titles witness, imperious and impatient to right the wrongs done to you, and where Rome has done you any harm, wreak triple satisfaction on Saturninus."

A Goth leader replied, "Brave scion, sprung from the great Titus Andronicus, whose name was once our terror, but is now our comfort, and whose high exploits and honorable deeds ungrateful Rome requites with foul contempt, have confidence in us. We'll follow wherever you lead us. We will be like stinging bees on the hottest summer's day led by their master to the flowered fields, and we will be avenged on cursed Tamora."

The other Goths said, "And as he speaks, so say we all with him."

"I humbly thank him, and I thank you all," Lucius said. "But who is coming here, led by a strong, powerful Goth?"

A Goth with a drawn sword led Aaron to Lucius. Aaron had his infant son in his arms.

The Goth who had taken Aaron prisoner said, "Renowned Lucius, from our troops I strayed to gaze upon a ruined monastery, and as I earnestly looked upon the destroyed building, suddenly I heard a child cry underneath a wall. I went to the noise, and soon I heard the crying babe calmed with this affectionate discourse: 'Peace, black slave, half me and half your mother! If only your hue had not betrayed whose brat you are, if only nature had lent you your mother's look, if only your skin color were white instead of black, villain, you might have been an Emperor. But when the bull and cow are both milk-white, they never beget a coal-black calf. Quiet, villain, quiet!' — and so he talked to the babe — 'For I must carry you to a trusty Goth, who, when he knows you are the Empress' babe, will treat you well for your mother's sake.'

"Hearing this, I drew my weapon and rushed upon him, surprised him suddenly, and brought him here so you can treat him as you think best."

65

Lucius replied, "Worthy Goth, this is the incarnate devil who robbed Titus Andronicus of his good left hand. This is the pearl that pleased your Empress' eye, and this babe here is the base fruit of his burning lust."

Lucius was referring to a proverb when he called Aaron a pearl: A black man is a pearl in the eyes of a fair woman.

He said to Aaron, "Say, glaring-eyed slave, where would you convey this growing image of your fiend-like face? Why don't you speak? What, are you deaf? Not a word will you speak to me? Bring a noose, soldiers! Hang him on this tree and by his side hang his fruit of bastardy."

"Don't touch the boy," Aaron said. "He is of royal blood."

"He is too much like the father to ever be good," Lucius said. "First hang the child, so that Aaron may see the child's death throes: a sight that will vex the father's soul."

Aaron, filled with bravado, said, "Get me a ladder."

A Goth brought a ladder, and Aaron climbed it. Some Goths tied a noose to a tree.

Aaron said, "Lucius, save the child, and carry it from me to the Empress. If you do this, I'll tell you wondrous things that may be highly to your advantage to hear. If you will not, then befall whatever may befall, I'll speak no more but 'May vengeance rot you all!'"

"Speak on, and if what you say pleases me, your child shall live, and I will see that it is taken care of," Lucius replied.

"And if what I say pleases you?" Aaron said. "Why, be assured, Lucius, what I have to tell you will vex your soul to hear because I must talk of murders, rapes, and massacres, acts of black night, abominable deeds, evil plots, treasons, villainies lamentable to hear and performed with full knowledge that they would cause people to feel pity. All of this shall be buried by my death, unless you swear to me my child shall live."

"Tell me what you have to say," Lucius said. "I say your child shall live."

"Swear that he shall live, and then I will begin."

"By whom should I swear? You believe in no god. That granted, how can you believe an oath?"

"So what if I do not believe in any god?" Aaron asked. "It is true, indeed, that I do not, but because I know that you are religious and have a thing within you called conscience, with twenty popish tricks and ceremonies that I have seen you being careful to observe, I therefore want your oath. If I know that an idiot fool regards his bauble — a jester's stick with a carved head on one end — as a god and keeps the oath that he swears by that god, then I would want him to make an oath. Therefore, you shall vow by that god, whatever god it is, whom you adore and hold in reverence, to save my boy, to nourish and nurse and bring him up — or else I will reveal nothing to you."

"By my god, I swear to you I will take care of your son," Lucius said.

"First know that I begot him on the Empress," Aaron said. "Tamora is my son's mother."

"She is a most insatiable and lecherous woman!"

"Tut, Lucius, this was but a deed of charity in comparison to that which you shall hear me tell you now. It was her two sons who murdered Bassianus. They cut out your sister's tongue and raped her and cut off her hands and trimmed her as you have seen."

"Detestable villain! Do you call that trimming?"

"Why, she was washed and cut and trimmed, and it was trim entertainment for them who had the doing of it."

The word "trim" has multiple meanings. "To trim" means "to prune" or "to cut." Lavinia had been pruned of her hands. "Trim" also had a sexual meaning in their society: A woman who has been trimmed is no longer a virgin. The "trim" entertainment enjoyed by Demetrius and Chiron was a sexual entertainment. Aaron's sentence also compared Lavinia to a piece of meat that was washed and cut and trimmed so that it could be cooked.

"Tamora's two sons are barbarous, beastly villains, like yourself!" Lucius shouted.

"Indeed, I was their tutor and instructed them. Their lecherous nature they inherited from their mother. She is like a high card guaranteed to win a game of cards; her lecherous nature guaranteed that their nature would be lecherous. The bloodthirstiness of their minds, I think, they learned from me. I am as true a dog as ever fought at head; I am like a bulldog that always attacks a bull head-on.

"Well, let my deeds be witness of my worth. I guided your brothers to that treacherous hole where the dead corpse of Bassianus lay. I wrote the letter that your father found, and I hid the gold that the letter mentioned. I was a confederate with the Queen and her two sons. What haven't I done that you have cause to rue? I always was involved in whatever has caused you grief. I cheated your father out of his hand, and, when I had his severed hand, I drew myself apart and almost injured my heart with extreme laughter — I nearly died from laughing. I was looking through the crevice of a wall when Titus, in exchange for his hand, received his two sons' heads. I saw his tears, and I laughed so heartily that both of my eyes were as rainy as his. And when I told the Empress about this entertainment, she almost swooned at my pleasing tale, and for my good news gave me twenty kisses."

The Goth leader said, "Can you say all this, and admit to doing all these evil deeds, and never blush?"

"I can blush like a black dog, as the common saying goes," Aaron replied.

"Aren't you sorry for committing all these heinous deeds?" Lucius asked.

"Yes, I'm sorry," Aaron replied. "I'm sorry that I have not done a thousand more evil deeds. Even now I curse the day — and yet, I think, few days come within the compass of my curse — wherein I did not do some notorious evil, such as kill a man, or else plan his death; rape a virgin, or plot the way to do it; accuse some innocent person and commit perjury; make two friends hate each other and wish the other to die; set snares to make poor men's cattle break their necks; set barns and haystacks on fire in the night, and tell the owners to quench the fires with their tears. Often I have dug up dead men from their graves, and set them upright at their dear friends' doors, at a time when their friends had almost recovered from sorrow, and on the dead men's skins, as if on the bark of trees, I have with my knife carved in Roman letters, *'Let not your sorrow die, although I am dead.'* Tut, I have done a thousand dreadful things as willingly as one would kill a fly, and nothing grieves me heartily indeed except that I cannot do ten thousand more dreadful things."

Lucius said, "Bring down the devil; for he must not die so sweet a death as hanging immediately."

Aaron climbed down from the ladder and said, "If there are devils, I wish I were a devil and would live and burn in everlasting fire, so that I might have your company in Hell and torment you with my bitter tongue!"

"Sirs, gag his mouth, and let him speak no more," Lucius said.

Some Goths gagged Aaron.

Another Goth walked over to Lucius and said, "My lord, a messenger has come from Rome and wants to be admitted to your presence."

"Let him come near," Lucius ordered.

A Goth brought Aemilius, the noble Roman who was serving as a messenger, to Lucius, who recognized him.

"Welcome, Aemilius. What's the news from Rome?"

"Lord Lucius, and you Princes of the Goths, the Roman Emperor sends all of you his greetings, and because he understands that you are armed and marching to Rome, he wants a parley with you at your father's house. If you want hostages to guarantee your safety, they shall be immediately delivered."

The Goth leader asked Lucius, "What does our general say?"

Lucius said, "Aemilius, let the Emperor give his pledges — the hostages — to my father and my uncle Marcus, and we will come."

He then ordered the Goths, "Let us march away."

— 5.2 —

Before Titus' house, Tamora and her two sons, Demetrius and Chiron, stood. They were dressed in fantastic costumes.

The disguised Tamora said, "Thus, in this strange and dark-colored costume, I will meet with Titus Andronicus, and tell him that I am Revenge, sent from below — the Land of the Dead — to join with him and right the heinous wrongs done to him.

"Knock at his study, where, they say, he stays and thinks about strange plots of dire revenge. Tell him that Revenge has come to join with him and work destruction on his enemies."

Demetrius and Chiron knocked on Titus' door.

Holding a document, Titus appeared at an upstairs window and asked, "Who molests my contemplation? Is this a trick to make me open the door so that my sad decrees may fly away, and all my study may be to no effect? You are deceived because what I intend to do you can see is here written in bloody lines I have set down; and what is written shall be executed."

"Titus, I have come to talk with you," Tamora replied.

"No, not a word," Titus replied. "How can I grace my talk when I lack a hand to gesture with? You have the advantage of me; therefore, say no more."

"If you knew who I am, you would talk with me," Tamora said.

"I am not mad; I know you well enough," Titus replied. "Witness this wretched stump, witness these crimson lines I have written with my blood in this document; witness these trenches — these wrinkles — made by grief and

69

care, witness the tiring day and dark night, witness all sorrow that I well know you are our proud Empress, mighty Tamora. Isn't your purpose for coming here to take my other hand?"

Tamora said. "Know, you sad and solemn man, I am not Tamora. She is your enemy, and I am your friend. I am Revenge, and I have been sent from the infernal kingdom to ease the gnawing vulture of your mind by working retributive vengeance on your foes.

"Come down, and welcome me to this world's light. Confer with me about murder and about death. There's not a hollow cave or lurking-place, no vast obscurity or misty valley where bloody murder or detested rape can hide for fear, but I will find them out; and in their ears I will tell them my dreadful name — Revenge, which makes the foul offender quake."

"Are you Revenge?" Titus asked. "And have you been sent to me to be a torment to my enemies?"

"I am; therefore, come down and welcome me."

"Do something for me, before I come to you," Titus said. "See by your side where Rape and Murder stand. Now give me some guarantee that you are Revenge. Stab them, or tear them on your chariot-wheels."

In this society, wheels were sometimes used to painfully kill people. One torture using a wheel was similar to that of the rack; people's bodies would be stretched on the wheel until the joints were dislocated or until one or more limbs were torn off. People who were to be broken on the wheel would be tied to a wheel, and their bones would be broken. They would then be left to die.

Titus continued, "Do this, and then I'll come and be your charioteer and whirl along with you about the globe. Provide two proper palfreys, as black as jet, to pull your vengeful wagon swiftly away, and find out murderers in their guilty caves, and when your chariot is loaded with their heads, I will dismount, and by the chariot wheel I will trot, like a servile footman, all day long, even from Sun's rising in the east until the Sun sets in the sea. And day by day I'll do this heavy and difficult task, as long as you destroy Rapine and Murder there."

Tamora replied, "These are my ministers, and they come with me."

"Are these your ministers?" Titus asked. "What are they called?"

The disguised Tamora, wanting to humor Titus, whom she thought was mad, used the same names that Titus had used earlier: "They are called Rape and Murder, and they are called those names because they take vengeance on men who rape and murder."

"Good Lord, how like the Empress' sons they are!" Titus said. "And how similar are you to the Empress! But we mortal men have miserable, mad, mistaking eyes.

"Sweet Revenge, now I come to you, and if one arm's embracement will content you, I will hug you with my one arm soon."

Titus exited from the window and started to climb downstairs.

"Titus' agreeing with what I say suits his lunacy — the madman believes me," the disguised Tamora said. "Whatever I invent to feed his brain-sick fits and moods, you, my sons, will uphold and maintain in your speeches because now he firmly believes that I am Revenge, and since he is credulous in this mad thought and amendable to accept suggestions, I'll make him send for Lucius, his son. Then, while I at a banquet have him securely in my control, I'll find some impromptu scheme to scatter and disperse the irresponsible Goths, or at least make them his enemies."

Titus began to open the door and Tamora said to her sons, "See, here he comes, and I must pursue my plot."

Titus said, "Long have I been pitifully lonely, and all because I wanted you, Revenge. Welcome, dread Fury, you goddess who pursues revenge, to my house that is filled with sorrows. Rape and Murder, you are welcome, too. How you resemble the Empress and her sons!

"Revenge, you would be well equipped if only you had a Moor. Could not all Hell lend you such a devil? For well I know the Empress never wags but in her company there is a Moor."

He thought, *When Tamora wags her tail, you can bet that the Moor is in bed with her.*

He continued, "And, if you would represent our Queen correctly, it would be fitting for you to have such a devil. But you are welcome as you are. What shall we do?"

"What would you have us do, Titus Andronicus?" the disguised Tamora asked.

"Show me a murderer, and I'll deal with him," Demetrius said.

"Show me a villain who has committed a rape, and I will exact revenge on him," Chiron said.

"Show me a thousand people who have done you wrong, and I will get revenge for you on all of them," Tamora said.

Titus said, "Look round about the wicked streets of Rome; and when you find a man who resembles yourself, good Murder, stab him — he's a murderer.

"Go with him, Rape, and when it is your luck to find another man who resembles you, good Rape, stab him — he's a rapist.

"Go with them, Revenge, and in the Emperor's court there you will find a Queen, who is attended by a Moor. You will recognize her by your bodily proportions because up and down she resembles you.

"Please, give these people a violent death; they have been violent to me and my loved ones."

"Well have you taught us," Tamora said. "This we shall do. But would it please you, good Titus Andronicus, to send for Lucius, your thrice-valiant son, who leads towards Rome a band of warlike Goths, and tell him to come and banquet at your house? When he is here at your ceremonious feast, I will bring in the Empress and her sons, as well as the Emperor himself and all the rest of your foes, and they shall be at your mercy and stoop and kneel, and on them you shall ease your angry heart.

"What do you say to this plan?"

Titus called, "Marcus, my brother! Sad and solemn Titus is calling you."

Marcus entered the room.

Titus said, "Go, kind and gentle Marcus, to your nephew Lucius. You will find him among the Goths. Tell him to come to me, and bring with him some of the most important Princes of the Goths. Tell him to have his soldiers camp where they are. Tell him that the Emperor and the Empress shall feast at my house, and he shall feast with them. Do this for me out of love for me, a love that I return, and so let him come here if he has any regard for his aged father's life."

"I will do this, and I will soon return again," Marcus said.

He exited.

Tamora said to Titus, "Now I will leave and go about your business, and I will take my ministers along with me."

"No, no," Titus said. "Let Rape and Murder stay with me, or else I'll call my brother back again, and cleave to no revenge except what Lucius shall get for me."

Tamora whispered to her sons, "What do you say, boys? Will you stay with him, while I go and tell my lord the Emperor how I have managed the jest we planned? Yield to Titus' moods, flatter and speak nicely to him, and stay with him until I return again."

Titus Andronicus thought, *I know them all, although they suppose me to be insane, and I will outwit them in their own plots. They are a pair of cursed Hell-hounds and their dam, aka mother!*"

Demetrius said to his mother, "Madam, depart when you like; leave us here."

"Farewell, Titus Andronicus," the disguised Tamora said. "Revenge now goes to lay a plot with which to betray your foes."

"I know you do," Titus replied, "and, sweet Revenge, farewell."

Tamora exited.

"Tell us, old man, how shall we be employed?" Chiron asked. "What do you want us to do?"

"Tut, I have work enough for you to do," Titus said. "Publius, come here, and Caius and Valentine come, too!"

Caius and Valentine were Titus' kinsmen; Publius was Marcus' son.

They entered the room, and Publius asked, "What do you want?"

Indicating Demetrius and Chiron, Titus asked, "Do you know these two men?"

Publius replied, "I think that they are the Empress' two sons: Chiron and Demetrius."

Titus said, "Really, Publius! You are too much deceived. One is named Murder, and the other is named Rape. Therefore tie them up, gentle Publius. Caius and Valentine, lay hands on them and keep them from running away. Often have you heard me wish for such an hour, one in which these two were in my control, and now I find it; therefore, bind them tightly, and gag their mouths if they begin to cry out."

He exited, and his kinsmen began to restrain and tie up Demetrius and Chiron.

Chiron shouted, "Villains, stop! We are the Empress' sons."

Publius replied, "And for that reason we do what Titus commands us to do."

He said to Caius and Valentine, "Gag their mouths, and don't let them speak a word. Make sure that you tie them securely."

Titus returned with Lavinia. He was carrying a knife, and she was carrying a basin with her stumps. Although her hands had been cut off at the elbows, she was able to carry the basin with her stumps by using her teeth to bite down on an edge of the basin.

"Come, come, Lavinia," Titus said. "Look, your foes are bound."

"Kinsmen, stop their mouths, don't let them speak to me. But do let them hear the words I utter — my words will cause dread and fear.

"Oh, you villains, Chiron and Demetrius! Here stands the spring — Lavinia — whom you have stained with mud. You mixed your winter with this good summer. You killed her husband, and for that vile crime two of her brothers were condemned to death and my hand was cut off and made a merry jest. You cut off both of her sweet hands as well as her tongue, and you inhuman traitors forcibly violated that which was dearer to her than her hands or tongue — her spotless chastity. What would you say if I should let you speak? Villains, for shame you could not beg for mercy and grace.

"Pay attention, wretches! Listen to how I mean to butcher you. This one hand is still left to cut your throats while Lavinia holds between her stumps the basin that will receive your guilty blood.

"You know your mother intends to feast with me, and calls herself Revenge, and thinks that I am insane. Pay attention, villains! I will grind your bones to fine powder and I will make pie dough with your blood and ground-up bones. Out of that dough I will make a piecrust that will be a coffin for the meat inside the pie — that meat will come from your shameful heads. Then I will tell that whore, your unholy dam, to swallow her own produce — her own children. She will be like the earth that first gives birth to us and then swallows us when we die and are buried in her.

"This is the feast that I have invited her to, and this is the banquet she shall glut on. You treated my daughter worse than Philomela was treated, and my revenge will be worse than that of Procne."

After Procne's husband, Tereus, raped her sister, Philomena, and cut out her tongue, Procne got revenge by killing the son she had had with Tereus, cooking him, and feeding him to Tereus.

Titus continued, "And now, Demetrius and Chiron, prepare for your throats to be cut. Lavinia, come and catch their blood."

Titus cut their throats, and Lavinia began catching their blood in the basin.

Titus said, "When they are dead, I will go and grind their bones to fine powder and with this hateful liquid mix it, and in that dough I will bake their vile heads.

"Come, come, everyone, be diligent in making this banquet, which I hope may prove to be sterner and bloodier than the Centaurs' feast."

When Pirithous, the King of the Lapiths, married Hippodamia, he invited the half-man, half-horse Centaurs to the wedding feast. The Centaurs got drunk, and tried to rape Hippodamia and carry away the Lapith women. Pirithous and the Lapiths fought back and defeated the Centaurs.

Titus said, "So, now bring their bodies inside my house, for I'll play the cook and see that they are ready to be eaten when their mother comes."

— 5.3 —

Lucius, Marcus, and some Goths arrived in the courtyard of Titus Andronicus' house. With them was Aaron, their prisoner. A Goth carried Aaron's son.

Lucius said, "Uncle Marcus, since my father wants me to come to Rome, I am happy to do so."

A Goth leader said, "We are also happy to do so, no matter what happens as a result."

Lucius said, "Good uncle, take this barbarous Moor, this ravenous tiger, this accursed devil, inside my father's house. Let him receive no food, but fetter him until he is brought before the Empress to give testimony of her foul proceedings. Also, see that our soldiers are prepared and ready to ambush enemy soldiers if needed. I fear that the Emperor means no good to us."

Aaron said, "I wish that some devil would whisper curses in my ear and prompt me so that my tongue could utter forth the venomous malice of my swelling heart!"

"Away with you, inhuman dog! Unholy slave!" Lucius said.

He ordered the Goths, "Sirs, help our uncle to convey him inside."

The Goths and Aaron exited.

Trumpets sounded.

Lucius said, "The trumpets show that the Emperor is very near."

Saturninus and Tamara, accompanied by Aemilius, some Tribunes, some Senators, and others, walked over to Lucius.

Saturninus said, "Has the firmament more Suns than one?"

Lucius replied, "How does it benefit you to call yourself a Sun?"

Marcus Andronicus said, "Rome's Emperor, and nephew, stop arguing. These quarrels must be quietly debated. The feast is ready that the sorrowful Titus has ordered for honorable reasons: for peace, for love, for alliance, and for good to Rome. Please, therefore, draw near, and take your places."

"Marcus, we will," Saturninus said.

Everyone sat down at a table, and Titus and Lavinia came into the courtyard. Titus was dressed like a cook and carrying dishes, and Lavinia was wearing a veil. With them were young Lucius and others.

Titus placed the dishes on the table.

He said, "Welcome, my gracious lord; welcome, revered Queen; welcome, warlike Goths; welcome, Lucius; and welcome, all. Although the food is poor, it will fill your stomachs; please eat."

"Why are you dressed like a cook, Titus Andronicus?" Saturninus asked.

"Because I wanted to be sure to have everything done well to entertain your Highness and your Empress."

"We are beholden to you, good Titus Andronicus," Tamora said.

"If your Highness knew my heart, you would be," Titus replied.

Titus' ironic remark meant this: If Tamora knew the trouble that he had gone to in order to serve her a meat pie and why he was serving it to her, she would know she owed him something — her life.

Tamora began to eat.

Titus then said, "My lord the Emperor, answer me this. Was it well done of the rash Virginius to slay his daughter, Virginia, with his own right hand because Appius Claudius had raped, stained, and deflowered her?"

"It was, Titus Andronicus," Saturninus replied.

"Your reason, mighty lord?"

"Because the girl should not survive her shame, and by her presence continually renew his sorrows."

"That is a reason mighty, strong, and conclusive," Titus said. "It is an example, precedent, and vivid authorization, for me, who is most wretched, to perform the same act."

Titus said, "Die, die, Lavinia, and let your shame die with you."

With full knowledge of what was to come, Lavinia deliberately ran to Titus, embracing both her father and the knife he used to kill her.

As Lavinia died, Titus lifted her veil and said, "And, with your shame dead, let your father's sorrow die!"

"What have you done, unnatural and unkind man!" Saturninus said. "Have you no love for your daughter?"

"I have killed my daughter, for whom my tears have made me blind," Titus said. "I am as woeful as Virginius was, and I have a thousand times more cause than he to do this outrage: and it now is done."

"What, was she raped?" Saturninus asked. "Tell us who did the deed."

"Will it please you to eat?" Titus asked. "Will it please your Highness to feed?"

Tamora asked, "Why have you killed your only daughter like this?"

"It was not I who killed her," Titus replied. "It was Chiron and Demetrius. They raped her, and cut out her tongue; and they — it was they who did her all this wrong."

Saturninus ordered some of his attendants, "Go and bring them here to us immediately."

Titus said, "Why, there they are both, baked in that pie, which their mother has been eating and enjoying. She has eaten the flesh that she herself has bred. It is true, it is true — my knife's sharp point is evidence that it is true."

Titus slit Tamora's throat and killed her.

"Die, frantic wretch, for this accursed deed!" Saturninus said as he drew his sword and killed Titus.

Lucius, Titus' only remaining living son, said as he drew his sword, "Can the son's eyes see his father bleed, and shall the son do nothing? There's meed for meed, measure for measure, and death for a deadly deed!"

Lucius killed Saturninus.

All was in tumult. The Goths ran to defend Lucius as the Romans ran to kill Lucius. The Romans thought that a coup was occurring and that Lucius had treacherously assassinated Saturninus and was attempting to become the new Emperor.

Lucius, Marcus Andronicus, young Lucius, and others went to the balcony.

Marcus Andronicus said to the Romans below the balcony, "You grave-looking men, people and sons of Rome, you have been separated by uproar like a flight of fowl that has been scattered by winds and high tempestuous gusts. You have been divided into factions. Oh, let me teach you how to knit again this scattered wheat into one mutual sheaf, how to knit again these broken limbs into one body."

An aged Roman replied, "Let Rome herself be poison to herself, and she whom mighty kingdoms curtsy to, like a forlorn and desperate castaway, execute shameful acts on herself."

From the aged Roman's point of view, Lucius had led an army of Goths into Rome and had murdered the Roman Emperor. In such a case, rather than being united with the Goths and ruled by Lucius, it might be better for Rome to destroy itself. After all, suicide can be preferable to loss of freedom.

The aged Roman continued, "But if my frosty white hair and wrinkles of old age, which are grave witnesses of true experience, cannot induce you to listen to my words, then speak, Marcus, you who as Tribune are Rome's dear friend, as previously our ancestor, Aeneas, spoke when with his solemn tongue he told love-sick Dido's attentive ears the story of that baleful, burning night when cunning Greeks ambushed King Priam's Troy through the stratagem of the Trojan Horse. Tell us what Sinon has bewitched our ears, or who has brought in the fatal engine — the Trojan Horse — that gives our Troy, our Rome, the wound of civil war."

The aged Roman wanted to know who had betrayed Rome by allowing the Goths inside the city. He wanted to know who was Rome's Sinon — Sinon was the treacherous Greek who convinced the Trojans to bring the Horse inside Troy. He had pretended that the Greeks wanted him dead, but he had escaped from them, and he told the Trojans about a false prophecy that stated that Troy would never fall if the Horse were brought inside the city. The Trojans themselves then brought the Horse inside the city, tearing down part of their defensive wall to do so.

Other relevant stories were the Rape of Philomela and the Rape of Lucrece. Following Lucrece's rape, she committed suicide, and the Romans deposed the King.

Marcus replied, "My heart is not composed of flint or steel, nor can I utter all our bitter grief because floods of my tears will drown my oratory and stop my speech, even in the times when what I say should move you to listen to me most attentively and force you to commiserate with me."

Pointing to Lucius, Marcus said, "Here is a captain. Let him tell the tale. Your hearts will throb and weep as you hear him speak."

Using the royal plural, Lucius said, "Then, noble listeners, know that cursed Chiron and Demetrius murdered Bassianus, our Emperor's brother. Also know that cursed Chiron and Demetrius raped Lavinia, our sister, and it is because of their terrible crimes that our brothers were beheaded, our father's tears despised, and he was basely cheated of that true hand that had fought Rome's war to its end and sent her enemies to the grave. Lastly, I myself was cruelly banished from Rome, the gates were shut on me, and I was turned weeping out to beg for relief among Rome's enemies, who drowned their hatred in my sincere tears and opened their arms to embrace me as a friend.

"I am the exile, you should know, who has protected Rome's welfare with my blood; I have sheathed the points of the enemy's weapons in my risk-taking body, diverting them from Rome's bosom. In my body, I have sheathed the enemy's steel.

"You know that I am no boaster. My scars can witness, although they cannot talk, that what I say is just and full of truth.

"But, wait! I think that I digress too much in talking about my worthless praise of myself. Oh, pardon me, for when no friends are nearby, men praise themselves."

Marcus said, "Now it is my turn to speak. Look at this child."

He pointed to the son of Aaron and Tamora; an attendant was holding the boy.

"Tamora delivered this child," Marcus said. "It is the child of an irreligious Moor who is the chief architect and plotter of these sorrows. The villain is alive in Titus' house, and he will give testimony that this is true.

"Now judge the reasons that Titus had to avenge these wrongs that are unspeakable, past all patience, more than any living man could bear.

"Now that you have heard the truth, what do you say, Romans? Have we done anything wrong? If so, show us, and from this high place where you see us now, the poor remaining Andronici will, hand in hand, all headlong jump and cast ourselves down and on the ragged stones below beat out our brains and bring the family of the Andronici to an end.

"Speak, Romans, speak; and if you say we should jump, then, hand in hand, Lucius and I will jump and fall."

Aemilius, a noble Roman, replied for the Romans, "Come, Marcus, come, you revered man of Rome, and bring our new Emperor gently in your hand — Lucius is our new Emperor — for I know well that he has popular support and the voices of the people say that he shall be Emperor."

The Romans shouted, "Lucius, all hail, Rome's royal Emperor!"

Marcus ordered some attendants, "Go into old Titus' sorrowful house, and bring that misbelieving Moor here so that he can be judged and given some dire and dreadful death as punishment for his most wicked life."

The attendants left to get Aaron, and Lucius, Marcus, young Lucius, and the others descended from the balcony.

The Romans shouted, "Lucius, all hail, Rome's gracious governor!"

"Thanks, noble Romans," Lucius said. "I hope that I may govern in such a way that will heal Rome's harms, and wipe away her woe! But, gentle people, bear with me for a while because nature gives me a heavy task. Everyone, stand back except you, uncle. You come nearer so that you can shed loving tears upon Titus' body."

Lucius kissed Titus' lips and said, "Take this warm kiss on your pale cold lips, these sorrowful drops upon your blood-stained face — the last true duties of your noble son!"

Marcus said to Titus' body, "Tear for tear, and loving kiss for kiss, Marcus, your brother, presents on your lips. Even if the sum of these kisses that I should pay you were countless and infinite, yet I would pay them!"

Lucius said to his son, "Come here, boy. Come, come, and learn from us how to melt in showers. Titus, your grandfather, loved you well. Many a time he danced you on his knee, and sang you asleep with his loving breast serving as your pillow. Many a story he has told to you, and told you to keep his pretty tales in your mind, and talk about them when he was dead and gone."

Marcus said to young Lucius, "How many thousand times have Titus' poor lips, when they were living, warmed themselves on your lips in kisses! Now, sweet boy, give them their final kiss! Tell your grandfather farewell, and commit him to the grave. Do his lips the kindness of kissing them, and take your leave of them."

Young Lucius said, "Oh, Grandfather, Grandfather! With all my heart, I wish that I were dead if it would make you live again!

"Oh, lord, I cannot speak to him because I am crying. My tears will choke me if I open my mouth."

The attendants returned with Aaron.

Aemilius said, "You sad Andronici, be done with your sorrows. Give this execrable wretch his sentence; he has been the breeder of these dire events."

Lucius ordered, "Bury him breast-deep in the earth, and starve him. There let him stand, and rave, and cry for food. If any person relieves or pities him, for that offence that person dies. This is our judgment.

"Some of you stay here to carry out our sentence and to see him buried breast-deep in the earth."

Aaron said, "Oh, why should wrath be mute, and fury not speak? I am no baby — not I. I am not one who with base, unworthy prayers will repent the evils I have done. I would do ten thousand evils worse than those I have done, if I could do what I want to do. If in all my life I did one good deed, I repent that good deed from my very soul."

Lucius said, "Some loving friends convey the late Emperor away from here, and give him burial in his fathers' grave. My father and Lavinia shall without delay be enclosed in our household's tomb. As for that heinous tiger, Tamora, she shall have no funeral rite and no man in mourning clothes, and no mournful bell shall ring her burial. Instead, throw her body to beasts and birds of prey. Her life was beast-like, and devoid of pity; and, being so, her body shall have a similar want of pity. See that our just sentence is carried out on Aaron, that damned Moor, by whom our heavy misfortunes had their beginning. We will then rule well the state, so that similar events never may destroy it."

A NOTE

In Shakespeare's play, both of Lavinia's hands are cut off and Titus' left hand is cut off. In this book, I write that they are cut off at the elbow.

Evidence for that include these things:

• Marcus talks about Lavinia's branches being cut off. (2.4)

• Titus says that he and Lavinia cannot fold their arms to express sorrow. (3.2)

• Titus says that Lavinia cannot thump on her chest. (3.2)

• Titus talks about not being able to gesture to grace his speech because he lacks a hand. If his hand and forearm are missing, that would make it hard for him to gesture. He could gesture oratorically much better if he had a forearm on the arm with the missing hand. (5.2)

• Titus talks about embracing Revenge, the disguised Tamora, with one arm. If he still had both forearms, he could embrace her with both arms. (5.2)

Evidence against the hands being cut off at the elbow — and rebuttals — include these things:

• Lavinia carries Titus' hand in her mouth. If this includes the forearm, it would be heavy. (3.1)

I think that Lavinia could do this. If necessary, she could use her stumps to help carry the hand.

• Lavinia uses her stumps to turn pages. (4.1)

It would be difficult, but Lavinia could turn pages without the use of her forearms. Also, she quickly gets help turning pages.

• Lavinia is able to use her stumps to guide Marcus' staff as she writes in the sand that Demetrius and Chiron raped her.

When Marcus comes up with the idea of writing in the sand and gives an example of doing that, he uses his feet to guide the staff as he writes. He may have done that because he thought that writing with upper arms only would be difficult. Besides, if Lavinia had forearms, she could use a forearm to write in the sand. (4.1)

• Lavinia uses her stumps to carry a basin. (5.2)

If the basin has handles on the side, she could use her mouth to bite on a handle and so carry the basin. Even if the basin lacks handles, she could bite on a side of the basin or put a side of the basin under her chin to help hold it steady.

83

Appendix A: About the Author

It was a dark and stormy night. Suddenly a cry rang out, and on a hot summer night in 1954, Josephine, wife of Carl Bruce, gave birth to a boy — me. Unfortunately, this young married couple allowed Reuben Saturday, Josephine's brother, to name their first-born. Reuben, aka "The Joker," decided that Bruce was a nice name, so he decided to name me Bruce Bruce. I have gone by my middle name — David — ever since.

Being named Bruce David Bruce hasn't been all bad. Bank tellers remember me very quickly, so I don't often have to show an ID. It can be fun in charades, also. When I was a counselor as a teenager at Camp Echoing Hills in Warsaw, Ohio, a fellow counselor gave the signs for "sounds like" and "two words," then she pointed to a bruise on her leg twice. Bruise Bruise? Oh yeah, Bruce Bruce is the answer!

Uncle Reuben, by the way, gave me a haircut when I was in kindergarten. He cut my hair short and shaved a small bald spot on the back of my head. My mother wouldn't let me go to school until the bald spot grew out again.

Of all my brothers and sisters (six in all), I am the only transplant to Athens, Ohio. I was born in Newark, Ohio, and have lived all around Southeastern Ohio. However, I moved to Athens to go to Ohio University and have never left.

At Ohio U, I never could make up my mind whether to major in English or Philosophy, so I got a bachelor's degree with a double major in both areas, then I added a Master of Arts degree in English and a Master of Arts degree in Philosophy. Yes, I have my MAMA degree.

Currently, and for a long time to come (I eat fruits and veggies), I am spending my retirement writing books such as *Nadia Comaneci: Perfect 10*, *The Funniest People in Dance*, *Homer's* Iliad: *A Retelling in Prose*, and *William Shakespeare's* Othello: *A Retelling in Prose*.

By the way, my sister Brenda Kennedy writes romances such as *A New Beginning* and *Shattered Dreams*.

Appendix B: Some Books by David Bruce

Retellings of a Classic Work of Literature

Arden of Faversham: *A Retelling*

Ben Jonson's The Alchemist: *A Retelling*

Ben Jonson's The Arraignment, or Poetaster: *A Retelling*

Ben Jonson's Bartholomew Fair: *A Retelling*

Ben Jonson's The Case is Altered: *A Retelling*

Ben Jonson's Catiline's Conspiracy: *A Retelling*

Ben Jonson's The Devil is an Ass: *A Retelling*

Ben Jonson's Epicene: *A Retelling*

Ben Jonson's Every Man in His Humor: *A Retelling*

Ben Jonson's Every Man Out of His Humor: *A Retelling*

Ben Jonson's The Fountain of Self-Love, or Cynthia's Revels: *A Retelling*

Ben Jonson's The Magnetic Lady, or Humors Reconciled: *A Retelling*

Ben Jonson's The New Inn, or The Light Heart: *A Retelling*

Ben Jonson's Sejanus' Fall: *A Retelling*

Ben Jonson's The Staple of News: *A Retelling*

Ben Jonson's A Tale of a Tub: *A Retelling*

Ben Jonson's Volpone, or the Fox: *A Retelling*

Christopher Marlowe's Complete Plays: Retellings

Christopher Marlowe's Dido, Queen of Carthage: *A Retelling*

Christopher Marlowe's Doctor Faustus: *Retellings of the 1604 A-Text and of the 1616 B-Text*

Christopher Marlowe's Edward II: *A Retelling*

Christopher Marlowe's The Massacre at Paris: *A Retelling*

Christopher Marlowe's The Rich Jew of Malta: *A Retelling*

Christopher Marlowe's Tamburlaine, Parts 1 and 2: *Retellings*

Dante's Divine Comedy: *A Retelling in Prose*

Dante's Inferno: *A Retelling in Prose*

Dante's Purgatory: *A Retelling in Prose*

Dante's Paradise: *A Retelling in Prose*

The Famous Victories of Henry V: *A Retelling*

From the Iliad *to the* Odyssey: *A Retelling in Prose of Quintus of Smyrna's* Posthomerica

George Chapman, Ben Jonson, and John Marston's Eastward Ho! *A Retelling*

George Peele's The Arraignment of Paris: *A Retelling*

George Peele's The Battle of Alcazar: *A Retelling*

George's Peele's David and Bathsheba, and the Tragedy of Absalom: *A Retelling*

George Peele's Edward I: *A Retelling*

George Peele's The Old Wives' Tale: *A Retelling*

George-a-Greene: *A Retelling*

The History of King Leir: *A Retelling*
Homer's Iliad: *A Retelling in Prose*
Homer's Odyssey: *A Retelling in Prose*
J.W. Gent.'s The Valiant Scot: *A Retelling*
Jason and the Argonauts: A Retelling in Prose of Apollonius of Rhodes' Argonautica
John Ford: Eight Plays Translated into Modern English
John Ford's The Broken Heart: *A Retelling*
John Ford's The Fancies, Chaste and Noble: *A Retelling*
John Ford's The Lady's Trial: *A Retelling*
John Ford's The Lover's Melancholy: *A Retelling*
John Ford's Love's Sacrifice: *A Retelling*
John Ford's Perkin Warbeck: *A Retelling*
John Ford's The Queen: *A Retelling*
John Ford's 'Tis Pity She's a Whore: *A Retelling*
John Lyly's Campaspe: *A Retelling*
John Lyly's Endymion, The Man in the Moon: *A Retelling*
John Lyly's Galatea: *A Retelling*
John Lyly's Love's Metamorphosis: *A Retelling*
John Lyly's Midas: *A Retelling*
John Lyly's Mother Bombie: *A Retelling*
John Lyly's Sappho and Phao: *A Retelling*
John Lyly's The Woman in the Moon: *A Retelling*
John Webster's The White Devil: *A Retelling*
King Edward III: *A Retelling*
Mankind: *A Medieval Morality Play* (A Retelling)
Margaret Cavendish's The Unnatural Tragedy: *A Retelling*
The Merry Devil of Edmonton: *A Retelling*
The Summoning of Everyman: *A Medieval Morality Play* (A Retelling)
Robert Greene's Friar Bacon and Friar Bungay: *A Retelling*
The Taming of a Shrew: *A Retelling*
Tarlton's Jests: A Retelling
Thomas Middleton's A Chaste Maid in Cheapside: *A Retelling*
Thomas Middleton's Women Beware Women: *A Retelling*
Thomas Middleton and Thomas Dekker's The Roaring Girl: *A Retelling*
Thomas Middleton and William Rowley's The Changeling: *A Retelling*
The Trojan War and Its Aftermath: Four Ancient Epic Poems
Virgil's Aeneid: *A Retelling in Prose*
William Shakespeare's 5 Late Romances: Retellings in Prose
William Shakespeare's 10 Histories: Retellings in Prose
William Shakespeare's 11 Tragedies: Retellings in Prose
William Shakespeare's 12 Comedies: Retellings in Prose
William Shakespeare's 38 Plays: Retellings in Prose

William Shakespeare's 1 Henry IV, aka Henry IV, Part 1: *A Retelling in Prose*

William Shakespeare's 2 Henry IV, aka Henry IV, Part 2: *A Retelling in Prose*

William Shakespeare's 1 Henry VI, aka Henry VI, Part 1: *A Retelling in Prose*

William Shakespeare's 2 Henry VI, aka Henry VI, Part 2: *A Retelling in Prose*

William Shakespeare's 3 Henry VI, aka Henry VI, Part 3: *A Retelling in Prose*

William Shakespeare's All's Well that Ends Well: *A Retelling in Prose*

William Shakespeare's Antony and Cleopatra: *A Retelling in Prose*

William Shakespeare's As You Like It: *A Retelling in Prose*

William Shakespeare's The Comedy of Errors: *A Retelling in Prose*

William Shakespeare's Coriolanus: *A Retelling in Prose*

William Shakespeare's Cymbeline: *A Retelling in Prose*

William Shakespeare's Hamlet: *A Retelling in Prose*

William Shakespeare's Henry V: *A Retelling in Prose*

William Shakespeare's Henry VIII: *A Retelling in Prose*

William Shakespeare's Julius Caesar: *A Retelling in Prose*

William Shakespeare's King John: *A Retelling in Prose*

William Shakespeare's King Lear: *A Retelling in Prose*

William Shakespeare's Love's Labor's Lost: *A Retelling in Prose*

William Shakespeare's Macbeth: *A Retelling in Prose*

William Shakespeare's Measure for Measure: *A Retelling in Prose*

William Shakespeare's The Merchant of Venice: *A Retelling in Prose*

William Shakespeare's The Merry Wives of Windsor: *A Retelling in Prose*

William Shakespeare's A Midsummer Night's Dream: *A Retelling in Prose*

William Shakespeare's Much Ado About Nothing: *A Retelling in Prose*

William Shakespeare's Othello: *A Retelling in Prose*

William Shakespeare's Pericles, Prince of Tyre: *A Retelling in Prose*

William Shakespeare's Richard II: *A Retelling in Prose*

William Shakespeare's Richard III: *A Retelling in Prose*

William Shakespeare's Romeo and Juliet: *A Retelling in Prose*

William Shakespeare's The Taming of the Shrew: *A Retelling in Prose*

William Shakespeare's The Tempest: *A Retelling in Prose*

William Shakespeare's Timon of Athens: *A Retelling in Prose*

William Shakespeare's Titus Andronicus: *A Retelling in Prose*

William Shakespeare's Troilus and Cressida: *A Retelling in Prose*

William Shakespeare's Twelfth Night: *A Retelling in Prose*

William Shakespeare's The Two Gentlemen of Verona: *A Retelling in Prose*

William Shakespeare's The Two Noble Kinsmen: *A Retelling in Prose*

William Shakespeare's The Winter's Tale: *A Retelling in Prose*

Mature Readers Only

The Erotic Adventures of Candide